MW01528230

To Heather,
My friend of
many years and
many more!
Love, Karla

Embroidered Life of Mine

by

Karla J. Gustafson

Karla J. Gustafson

2005

authorHOUSE™

1663 LIBERTY DRIVE, SUITE 200
BLOOMINGTON, INDIANA 47403
(800) 839-8640
WWW.AUTHORHOUSE.COM

© *2005 Karla J. Gustafson. All Rights Reserved.*

First published by AuthorHouse 04/04/05

ISBN: 1-4208-3343-X (sc)

Library of Congress Control Number: 2005902330

Printed in the United States of America
Bloomington, Indiana

This book is printed on acid-free paper.

Dedicated to my Mom.
For helping me so much with everything.

The future is something that hasn't happened yet. Something that hasn't happened yet, can always be changed.

Table of Contents

Part One

Poems 3
twist 7
and 10
turn 14
to.. 17
make 21
a 24
curve..27
Life..32
flies...35
by 39
like 42
a 45
page..47
that's..50
turned 53

Part Two

Poems 65
twist 70
and 74
turn 78
to.. 82
make 84
a 89
curve..93

Life 97
flies 103
by 107
like 109
a 112
page 115
that's 118
turned 121

Poems twist and turn
to make a curve.
Life flies by like a page
that's turned.

Part One

New York City, U.S.A.

"My life is embroidered out for me in one straight line."

Chapter 1

Poems

It was like any other day. I went to classes, was a good student, was a good girl. Always doing the right thing. Inside I was screaming, saying everything that would shame me for sure.

My name is Lacy Slucipher. I like to think I am part devil, it is better than being full angel. That's what my parents thought.

I was sent to "Missionara – Private Academy for Young Ladies", a private school in New York City for the daughters of American Missionaries. I first attended the Academy in 1904 when I was twelve, after my parents died on a missionary trip over in Africa. They were bitten by a poisonous insect one day and dead the next. I had been living with my Great Aunt Selma while they were away that year. I would never forget the day I found out my parents had died, it was like a giant foot stepping on my life.

Then, shortly after my parents death and once I had started school, Aunt Selma died. I never did like her much, she never seemed to like my parents or I either for that matter. She and my mother always seemed to be talking about something that would get them both in a tizzy, then we wouldn't visit her for a year or two after they had argued.

I think the only nice things about my aunt were when she took me in to live with her, paying for my schooling and in her Will, leaving her fortune to me. What seems weird is that she didn't leave it to my parents, since she made her final draft long before they died. Well, anyway, if it weren't for her I wouldn't have any money at all. Missionary people are very poor.

Now I am fifteen with only a few months left before my next birthday, and am very ignorant. I have long auburn hair and red lips. My eyes are blue, nothing more than blue. I think the only other physical feature I like about myself besides my lips, would have to be my butt. It is nicely rounded, but doesn't stick out too far. Of course no one else knows that, it wouldn't be proper.

I live at the Academy with fifty other girls, ages twelve to eighteen. Across the courtyard is the Academy for Young Men. There are forty boys between the ages of twelve and eighteen also.

These Academies are not your ordinary orthodox private schools. A lot of missionary kids go to these types of schools because they have lived their life all around the world and think in a more modern way than others. You couldn't just throw kids like me, who have seen things that ordinary kids would never see, into the usual American schools. It just wouldn't work. So, there are still numerous rules to obey, but they are not as "thin minded" as the other schools around. Missionary kids are very advanced in their learning, so most of us can graduate two or three years before the "normal" kids do.

The boys from across the way come over every Friday for afternoon tea. It is delightful to be near the opposite sex. I get so tired of all the other girls' emotions. They are all worried that they will never get married, except they all do.

I share a room with three other girls around my age. Emma, who is absolutely beautiful. She is engaged to Billy and they make a lovely couple. Tabitha, or Tabby as we all call her, is my best friend and has the most beautiful long, curly, blonde hair you'll ever see. Then there's Rachel, who is just quiet and only talks when spoken to, which is proper and how young ladies are supposed to act, but it always seems a little strange. She's even that way when there are no adults around. Also, there's our friend Dorothy who is in the room right next to ours. She has a temper like a hornet, but is still our friend never the less.

Each day we are educated in reading, writing, some arithmatic and French. I don't know why they are so keen on us learning the language, it's not like any of us will ever be over in France. Also, every day after tea we spend three hours embroidering, sewing, knitting and such like that. I like doing all those things, just not for three hours. I don't have much patience and my attention span seems to decrease some every year.

So, while the teacher speaks some foreign language and calls off numbers, I get lost somewhere in a day dream. A dream that will never come true. If I had wings I would fly away from this place. What more do they have to teach me? The only reason for a private school in the first place, is to teach girls, pardon me, young ladies to be good wives. To be able to take care of their children and husbands. The majority believe women are on this earth for one reason and one reason only, that is to bring pleasure to their husbands and households. If that was God's plan, then why do women have brains and thoughts?

Chapter 2

twist

"Lacy, wake up, wake up!" Through my clouded eyes I could see Tabby hovering over me. "Lacy, wake up, Caitlina is having one of her fits again, she needs you."

Though weak and tired I got out of bed and put my robe on. With an angry tone I asked, "Where is she?"

"She's in her room and screaming to heaven high."

I took a deep breath and stared at Tabby. In a whispered voice she said, "You know you are the only one who can calm her down."

"I know," I muttered. I stumbled to Caitlina's room and stood in the doorway looking at her, she is just twelve and very small. Her parents were killed right in front of her, shot by two bank robbers out West. Caitlina is the wealthiest girl at our school. She inherited all her parents money, so she has the biggest room out of everyone. It is beautiful, looks like the room came straight from a palace of a princess of India. Rich colors of gold, everywhere you look, and jewels hanging from beautiful ivory elephant tusks. She came here a year ago, right after her parents died. Ever since then she'll have a major fit of kicking and screaming about every two weeks. For some reason I'm the only one who can calm her down.

I think it's because my parents died when I was her age and I can talk about it. The other girls who have lost their parents just say they died and that's the end of the story. No feeling, no emotion. Just died one day and life continued the same.

As I stood there looking at this wild and angry child, I realized that she wasn't a child anymore. There it was, spilled on the bed, the growing part that decides when we become a woman. Red blood. I walked lightly over to her bedside and sat on the edge. I fingered through her hair like I had always done to let her know I was there for her. I spoke softly, "Caitlina."

She looked up at me through her red, hot face and swollen, tear stained eyes, then hid them with her pillow.

"Honey, I , I, look at me please."

"What?" she seemed confused.

"Caitlina, you are not a little girl anymore. You see this blood on your sheet? Well, this blood says you are no longer a child. You are a young lady, a young woman." I smiled at her, not sure how she would respond.

She smiled, but then her smile turned into a full scream, "I'm not a woman! My mama's dead!"

"Yes Caitlina, your mother is dead, but you are a young woman. Here, let me show you something." I lifted a pillow up so I could sit Caitlina up to show her my treasure. "See," I said, holding a locket open with a picture of my mother in it. She smiled. "This is my mother, and you know what? She wasn't here either when I became a woman, but I am one, and so are you. We can be women together."

She looked up at me with wonderous eyes, then smiled. She said slowly, "I guess if I were a child forever, I wouldn't be able to get married and have a family."

"That's right," I told her.

She took a deep breath then said in a sober way, "This isn't going to be easy".

"No, it isn't, but I will help you. I promise you." I left with a good feeling of relief. I think now that she's a woman things won't be as hard. Or maybe even harder. Great!

Chapter 3

and

"Miss Slucipher, would you like a tea cake with your afternoon tea?"

"No, no my good man, I have a deadline to meet by this afternoon. Please hold all my callers."

"Miss Slucipher. Miss Slucipher!" I felt a hard poke in my ribs from Dorothy when I turned my head from the window to see Mr. Cambell looking boldly at me. He is quite an ugly man, short and fat, with no hair left except on his arms.

"Miss Slucipher, for the fourth time, what is 3 x-(2r)2?"

"Aaaa, I do not know sir."

"Well, maybe if you were paying attention like you should be, instead of day dreaming, you would know the answer."

And maybe if you weren't so boring I could pay attention, I thought. "Yes sir," I answered while putting my head down. I tried to care about my studies and mostly I did good in my classes. Except arithmatic, it did not make any sense and was just useless for what I wanted to do with my life.

I was day dreaming about being a famous poetry writer, like Emily Dickenson. I would be in a grand hotel and everyone would want my autograph. All the single young men would be calling on me to have tea with them. I wanted to be an author more than anything. A poetry author. The only person who had ever seen my poetry was Tabby. She says I have a "real gift" for writing poems about life and feelings. That is why I have asked my English teacher, Mrs. Mansen, to read some of my poems and tell me what she thinks of them. My heart is racing at the thought of her disliking them. Out of all the teachers at my school, she seemed to be the most likely one to really tell me if my poems were good or not. But I'm afraid that could be a bad thing.

Today the sun was way too hot. Yellow and white streams of light came pouring through the windows that lined the room, I had to squint to see the chalkboard. Problem after problem written on the board. How was I ever to understand arithmatic? It was useless, I might as well give up now before I wasted all my time trying.

"Miss Slucipher, I would like to see you after class," said Mr. Cambell sternly, sitting at his desk.

I let out a sigh as I gathered my books and paper, and walked to my death sentence.

"See you later," Dorothy said as she passed me on the way out of class.

I walked up to Mr. Cambell's desk and stood there looking down at whatever it was he was writing. It looked like he was adding up my test scores. Just what I need, both numbers and people telling me how dumb I am.

"Miss Slucipher, I do not think I have to tell you this but will," he paused, stopped writing and looked up at me with his huge, overly sized eyes. "You are failing Arithmatic. I am afraid you will have to repeat this class next term."

Oh, is that all, I thought. Now I get to be with Mr. Cambell another whole term! Why does my life go this way? "Yes sir," I said and he waved a hand saying I could leave. I walked solemly down the hallway, up the stairs, and down more hallways until I got to my room. It was there I put my books in their place, classes were over for the day and I felt dead inside. Tired and weak even though I had been just sitting mostly all day, I headed down to dinner where I ate in silence. The silence in the dining room matched the silence in my head. Perfect fit.

As bedtime approached time seemed to slow down and my eyes wandered with each passing person. We each knelt by our beds and said our prayers. Then lay down and hoped to be the first asleep, before someone started snoring, keeping you up the whole night.

I'm dreaming. *I am crying and running along a smooth dirt path. I stop and my hair is sticking to my face from my sweat. There's a long snake in the high bananna tree, it is coiled on a branch. Colors of its scales are highly rich patterns of sun yellow and fever red. I start to laugh but it turns into a cry, tears washing down my face, I start running again.*

Out of breath, I stop by a rocky hill, at the bottom there is a pond of fresh water. I can barely breathe from all the spit in my mouth. I kneel down to drink the water from the pond. My face is close to the water when I pull back to look at the water more closely. It is my mother's face. She is washed out, but it is her. "Mother," I call. Her smile goes away and so does she. I am frightened and confused. Splashing my hand through the water trying to find her face again. I cut water in my hand to try and see her face, but I do not.

The water in my hand turns red, it is blood that is thick and has an appalling odor to it. I throw the water out of my hand and back into the pond. Each drop that comes from my hand slowly turns the crystal clear pond water into darkening blood. I cannot see my reflection anymore. My head is light and so is my entire body, I feel like I could float away. I fall back into the mixture of blood and water. Then I am gone.

Chapter 4

turn

Our room was hot, sticky and I could feel the sweat slipping down my back. I felt gross and wished that I could take a long, cold bath with ice cubes in the water with me. How nice it would feel.

"This corset is killing me, I can hardly breathe," I said with a gasp.

"Come now Lacy, the gentlemen are going to be here any minute for tea and your hair isn't fixed," Tabby said, as if she was not nervous at all.

"You mean boys. Those gentlemen you call them, never seem too gentle," I said, so sure of myself, not ready for the next remark coming.

"Oh Lacy, you poor girl. You have to be with a man before you can call him gentle or not," said Margot. Rumor had it that last summer when she went home to see her beau they did a lot more than just talk. Margot was known for her "aggressive ways" with men and I think her parents just sent her way out here to New York so they wouldn't have to accept her shame.

"Shut up Margot, at least I'm not you. Your parents practically disinherited you." After that I felt cold, even though it was ninety degrees outside. She made me so mad.

Margot shot her nose up and mumbled, "virgin girl", all the way down the hall.

"Never mind her Lacy. Well, your hair looks just beautiful and I love that royal blue sash you are wearing," Tabby chattered. Through all the commotion in talking to Margot I had no idea Tabby had been doing my hair the whole time. It came as quite a shock when she said it was done.

"Thanks Tabby. Umm Tabby?"

"Yes?"

"Do you like these teas we have with the boys?"

"Sure, why?"

"Well, I just feel like I'm some animal put out on display, and the boys decide which girls to keep and which ones to throw out," I exclaimed with a worried look on my face.

"That's not true," Tabby assured me. "Now, come on. Mrs. Talbee will be mad if we are late."

I still wasn't satisfied. "Uhm, you go ahead, I'll be right down." I could tell my voice gave as I spoke. Tabby looked at me as if waiting for me to say something more. What was there to say? Then she turned and walked away. After she was gone, I stood in front of the mirror looking at myself. I was tall, medium sized and my hair was in a curly mess of a bun. My dress was shades of whites and tans with a royal blue sash around the waist. I felt like a porcelain doll, one that only moves when a child plays with it.

All the girls at our school are porcelain dolls. All the ladies of our society are porcelain dolls. I won't be forever a doll that is controlled. I promise myself that.

As I was about to walk out of our room I noticed that we had left the window open. Yes, the air was better outside than inside, but soon the bugs would be out, and I refused to sleep in a mosquito filled room. Can you say, getting eaten alive? Also, ever since my parents died from a mysterious bug bite, I have been more cautious. Bugs carry so many diseases, I learned that from Mrs. Talbee.

I walked across our room to close the window before going down. The window was a very pretty one at that. It had rose leaves printed or pressed into the brass metal frame. As I reached up to close the window, I peered down onto the lawn. There, behind a dogwood tree, full in bloom, I saw Emma and Billy. Kissing. Those two, thinking they could hide behind a tree, I must admit, it was quite romantic. I felt envious, really. Closing the window and turning to go down to tea, I let out a sigh of yearning.

Chapter 5

to

My hand slid down the oak railing and my back was straight. I could see all the pupils visiting and nervously flirting. We would all socialize for about half an hour, then sit down to tea. Maxium to a table was four people, two girls and two boys. It was even that way. Also, if there were two individuals who were courting they would sit just by each other. Or if it was an uneven number, you may end up sitting with just one other person. I hoped I never ended up sitting alone with a boy. It would be so ackward and oh how the girls would talk. You could barely look at a boy without getting malarky from the other girls. It was really rotten.

The parlor was always beautifully decorated. The chairs had red satin seats and the tables were a mother of pearl color, and always polished sparkly. The great chandelier above was elegant to the extreme and had crystals hanging from it. Not real crystals of course, but so beautiful just the same. I felt like a queen and peasant all at the same time. The wooden floors were freshly mopped and the wood grain looked like veins of deep colors running through the wood. Much like in a human, not that we're wood or anything.

As I got closer to the group in the sitting room my heart started beating wildly and I got very hot and sweaty. Being sweaty and red in the face was just what I needed now, when I was already nervous. Luckily, I had spent so much time looking at myself in the mirror that it was pretty much tea time once I got down there. Good, I really didn't feel like socializing. Mrs. Talbee told me once that I really should work on my social skills. She said, "How else will you find yourself a man dear?" How does she know if I want a man or not. But of course to be respectful I just nodded my head and replied "yes ma'am," and that was the end of that.

I was one of the last into the parlor where the tea was being served. I noticed that all the tables were full. Great, now what was I supposed to do? Drink my tea standing up! I scanned the room with my eyes, thinking for sure there was a place for me. There was always a place for everyone. Finally, after everyone was seated I noticed one of the side tables had an empty seat. As I walked to the table I felt all eyes on me. That was not something that usually happened and I hoped for it never to happen again. When I got to the table I accepted the fact that it was a two seater table and asked in the most patient and respectful voice I could find in myself, "Is this seat taken?"

The young man looked up. I knew him, I had known him for the last three years. I had seen him many times from afar. He had changed in appearance so much from the early weeks of this school year until now that I hardly recognized him. He had blonde hair and deep blue-green eyes hidden behind hideous glasses. He stood up right away when he realized I was talking to him, seeming rather surprised. He was very tall, taller than me by at least seven inches, and thin. He stammered as he spoke his words, "N-no."

I smiled and sat down with a new nervous feeling that hadn't been there before. Umm, it looked like we had gotten new teacups, blue birds were painted on the sides and the handle was a creamy white. Better than the plain white teacups we had last year. We drank our tea in silence, listening to everyone else laughing and having a jolly time. I just couldn't take our silence anymore, "Excuse me, but I do not think I caught your name."

"I'm Lief, Lief Phelpsson," he smiled, embarrassed. Then spoke again, "I am Swedish." He didn't stutter this time. He took another drink of tea then looked up and asked in a more confident way, "What is your name?"

"Lacy, Lacy Slucipher," I answered. He smiled and took another drink of tea. I must say his smile was breathtaking. It was beautiful but aggravating at the same time.

His next question was not very seemly for two people who had just met. He asked, "What would you want to be if you didn't have to get married?"

"Excuse me," I asked, with a stunned tone in my voice and heart.

"What would you be if you didn't have to get married," he repeated.

Now I was fully agitated. I blurted out, "What do you mean if I did not have to get married? How do you know what I can or cannot do?"

He looked astonished but said, "Well, women are expected to get married and make their husbands happy." Lief just said everything I have always known, but for some reason I didn't want to hear it out of his mouth. I was mad and frustrated, and I wasn't going to keep it in. Like I had done my whole life.

"Well, men are supposed to cheat on their wives, but that does not make it right!" After I said that I knew I had said too much, but so had he.

"I'm sorry." His pale cheeks flushed red.

I felt terrible because I knew he really was sorry. "No, no, I, I'm sorry," now I was the one stuttering. I looked down at my teacup and stirred the tea with my spoon. I knew I had to say more. I looked up at him with nervous eyes, "You are right you know, what you said is true and I know that. I just, I just didn't want to hear it from anyone else but myself."

He looked up, smiled and stared into my eyes like he was searching for something. He could see right through me, into my being. "So," he looked down at his tea, "what do you want to be?"

I looked up at him wondering why he cared what I thought and wanted. "Umm," I took a breath, "I want to be an author, a poetry writer." He looked at me the same way as before that made me feel naked.

"Could I read some of your poems?"

"Well, they are personal. I take them seriously."

"As do I," he sincerely replied.

I looked deep in his eyes and tried to look through to his heart. I wanted to make sure he was true before I let him read my most personal thoughts. Then, made a decision, "Okay."

Chapter 6

make

I left Lief sitting there while I went up to my room to get a few of my poems for him to take back home with him. I felt nervous as I handed them to him, they are the core of who I am, the center of my being. But, I had already said yes and I would not go back on my word. We both agreed that he would give them back next Friday at tea.

When tea was over and all of us were going to our rooms to take off those tight corsets, both Caitlina and Tabby were overwhelming me with questions about "the boy I was talking with the whole time during tea." I couldn't help but smile. Hopefully to get them off my back, I told them everything we had talked about, from weather, books, politics, etc. I lied. We hadn't talked about any of those things. But how could I tell them the things we talked about? They wouldn't understand and besides it really was none of their business. They were my good friends, but they could be so annoying.

"Why, virgin Mary, who was that I saw you talking with down at tea," asked a snarly voice. I took a deep breath and turned around to see Margot. Of course, when the day is good it has to be ruined some way or another.

"What do you want Margot?" All the girls backed me up except for a few who were her posse.

"Nothing, virgin girl, I already had it all." She smiled in an evil way, her only way.

"Shut up Margot. Why don't you just leave Lacy alone, she never did anything to you. You are nothing Margot, nothing but trash." I stood there with my mouth wide open. Everyone's mouth's were open, even Margots! Rachel had said all those things in defending me, quiet, sweet Rachel. She had never spoken out like that before.

I smiled and put my arm on Rachel's shoulder and gave her a little squeeze for a thank you. Margot, speechless for once, just turned and walked away. As she turned she tripped on her long shawl that was dragging on the floor. Her hair fell to a mess and her "posse" hurried to help her up, then scampered off with Margot in pieces. I think Margot was more surprised Rachel had spoken like that, than hurt from falling. Once we got back to the bedroom I just had to ask Rachel a question that had bothered me for years. "Rachel, why don't you talk much?"

She looked back at me in her shy way and answered simply, "There was never anything important enough to speak my mind about."

I could tell I wasn't going to get a bigger answer, so I gave a nod and left it at that. Rachel went over to her bedside and started to change into her nightgown, then took out her book she reads a lot, "*The Selected Poems of Emily Dickenson*". I will give her credit, she had good taste in poets. Emily Dickenson was one of my favorite poets, along with Walt Whitman.

Night comes and I'm afraid of dreams. Dreams that never come true, dreams that don't make sense, dreams that seem so real. I'm in a dream.

There are negros all around me. Their faces seem to be hidden though. There is a blurry spot in front of each of their faces. I'm frustrated. I rub my eyes wildly trying to clear my vison, I want to be able to see their faces. I can't.

There are grass huts everywhere, with deer skins hanging to cover the entryways. There are long speers, freshly carved, leaning against each of the huts making me shudder. The dirt smells clean, at least compared to the people.

A little boy with his bare chest and buckskin covering runs past me. I turn in all directions trying to see where he has gone. He is nowhere and no one seems to be looking for him.

There is a heavenly, obese woman selling baskets. I try to ask her where I am and why everyone's face is blurred out, but I can't talk. My throat is getting caught up with itself and I can no longer talk, I can no longer see.

Everything has gone dark and I stumble around searching for something to hold on to, there's nothing. I stumble and whine what little sound will come out of my mouth.

I'm knocked down, I have hit something hard and strong. My head is spinning and I feel like my whole body is being stretched out to cover the earth.

And then I'm gone.

Chapter 7

a

"Spell complicated," I say.

"Umm, c-o-m-p-l-i-c-a-t-e-d, right?"

"Correct!"

We are having a big spelling bee in a few days and we're studying like crazy for it. It was a combination of all the words we had learned over the years.

"Okay," said Tabby, with a sly tone in her voice and a wild smile on her face, "spell", she paused, then looked up from the list of words, "recapitulate." Tabby smiled again with a sly expression.

"What? I don't even know what it means!" We both started laughing and Tabby grabbed a dictionary out from where our school books were stored under our beds, and started to look up the meaning.

There was a knock on our door and it was opened. "Lacy, Mrs. Mansen wants to see you," Dorothy said in her "always hating the world" tone.

My heart stopped. I knew it was about my poems. What she said could affect my future. I walked slowly down the hallway to Mrs. Mansen's classroom. I still had time to run. I could get a job for washing rich peoples clothes and hide out under bridges so I wouldn't get caught during the day. I could steal food if I couldn't afford it, but always to ask God's forgiveness at the end

of the day. I still had time to do those things and not
face what I had been waiting so long for. When I got
to the door I took a deep breath, then knocked lightly
on the door.

"Come in," I heard a strong voice say. Blast, I'd
had my chance but now it was gone. I stepped in the
doorway to see Mrs. Mansen sitting at her desk going
through my poems. I walked over to her desk and stood
in front of her. Her room was neat and tidy, like her.

"Miss Slucipher, I have read your poems," she said
in a clipped voice.

My mind raced and I thought, thanks for stating
the fact but what did you think of them?

"Lacy your poems are fine, but dear, this should only
be a hobby of yours. You can have dreams, that's good,
but they will only ever be dreams. Your job is going
to be getting married and taking care of your husband
and children. That is your duty, that is why you were
put on this earth." She said it all with a pleasant smile
on her face, as if that would make it better.

All I could do was nod my head and turn away and
leave. Once I got back to my room, Tabby smiled wide
as I entered the room and spoke lightly, "recapitulate,
it means to summarize." I didn't care and felt sick and
extremely embarassed from what Mrs. Mansen had
just said. I burst into tears and hit my pillow. It wasn't
fair, nothing was fair when you're a woman. Why
couldn't my dreams be real? Aren't I real? Oh no!, I
thought. If Mrs. Mansen didn't like my poems, then
what would Lief think? I have now officially made a
jackass of myself.

"Lacy, are you okay," Tabby asked with total shock on her face.

I continued crying. Tabby came over and sat down on the side of my bed. She didn't say anything more, knowing I was too upset to talk about it, but started to rub my back in comfort. Tabby was really the best friend ever, she was like my sister. I couldn't ask for a better friend. Thank God for her.

Chapter 8

curve

It was the day of Emma Bradley's wedding. Everyone was in a frazzled mess, making sure her dress was perfect, the flowers still fresh and that Billy Craw did not get a sneak peak of her before the ceremony. I, although excited for Emma and Billy, just wanted to shrivel up and die. I didn't want to be seen, I was still mortified and embarrassed about my poems. That I even let Lief read them, Mrs. Mansen too.

Emma was the most beautiful bride that I had ever seen. Actually she was the only bride I had ever seen, but still the most beautiful ever I'm sure. Her dress was snow white with lace lining the neck and bodice. She wore her hair up in a tight bun, a veil fell over her face and back down her back. It was breathtaking.

Everyone had gone down to the chapel, taking their nervous chatter and opinions with them. Emma and I were alone in her bedroom with only minutes left before her marriage would take place.

"Are you nervous?" I asked, looking at her through her veil.

She smiled her beautiful smile and spoke in an angelic tone of voice, "I am marrying the man I have dreamed of my whole life." She paused then looked back at me, "I am a bit nervous though." She giggled and was her old self again. We both giggled, and then I left her alone. She would be getting married soon.

"Do you take this man to be your lawfully wedded husband?" The minister spoke with a sweet smile upon his old wrinkled face.

"I do," came the sure reply.

It wasn't a very warm day for mid Spring, but not too cold either. The sky seemed grayish, but it was a blessed change from the unusually hot weather we had been having. As the ceremony ended and we made our way into the reception room I couldn't help but look around for Lief. In some ways I wanted to see him again, but in other ways I didn't want to face him.

Emma's wedding cake was five layers high and had beautiful pink roses all over it. Everyone was dancing, laughing and having a great time. Except me. I decided to leave early, maybe go and study some for the spelling bee. I wasn't falling behind so much in spelling as I was in arithmatic. But spelling made more sense than arithmatic did, at least to me. As I walked across the yard, the fog fell in and the grass became covered in dew. I walked straight and tall, although I felt small and shriveled.

"Lacy, Lacy wait," came a yell from behind me. I stopped and looked back. It was Lief. He wore a nice black suit with a tie and cumberbun. My heart leaped and suddenly I hoped my hair looked okay. As he came up to me I straightened my dress and bit my lips to make them red.

"Hello," he said with his beautiful smile, then he looked confused. "Aren't you staying?"

"No, I thought I might go and study. We have a spelling bee tomorrow."

"Oh," he said with a disappointed look on his face. Then he started up again, "Well I wanted to give your poems back."

He paused and my heart stiffened, getting ready for the worst. "Your poetry is very good. He paused again and had a loss of words. My heart relaxed some.

"I've never read anything so deep, I think you will be an excellent author," he said quietly.

I blushed and smiled. How do I respond to that? "Thank you." I turned to go.

"Wait! Don't you want to know which one was my favorite?"

"Oh, yes of course."

"Here, sit down," he waved his hand to a stone bench in the center of the courtyard. The flowers were in bloom but looked cold with the dew sitting on them. They looked tired, like after a long day at classes when no one seemed to pay any attention to you. I sat down gently, and he sat next to me.

"I was wondering what this poem was about?" He started to read it.

"Dearest,
I have gone away
passed on to the dead
I hopefully didn't
leave anything in dread
I have seen the sun
rise and fall
I have seen the moon

cradled in the gloom
But your face I will
never see again
And that is what pains
me to the end."

He looked up at me. "Who is this about?"

I took a gulp and thought of what to say. "Well, it's not really about anyone in particular. It's kind of about my parents. They died when I was twelve and I will never see them again. Well, at least for a while," I said in an ever quieting voice.

"Oh. I'm sorry." He folded the paper with the poem and gave it back to me. "Well, my favorite poem of yours is probably this one." He started reading.

"Dear Life
that I have not known
Please stand by and wait
for me alone
Help me through
the hard times
When I feel so
bethroned
And carry my soul
away to the great
Unknown."

"It's so honest," he smiled and gave me the paper. I took it and looked up at Lief, who was already staring at me.

"Lacy," he said in a whisper, "you have beautiful eyes." It was a suprising thing to hear, but what came next was a bigger surprise. He leaned over and kissed me! Right on the lips! It was soft, delicate and quick. I felt my pulse race.

"Can I call on you this evening?" he asked with a softness in his voice.

"Yes." It all happened so quickly, it was such a tender exchange.

Chapter 9

Life

Late in the afternoon Emma and Billy left on their wedding trip to Boston and would be back in a weeks time. Emma planned to finish out the last month of the school year after their wedding trip, then she and Billy would set up house keeping on their own. Emma's father paid for their wedding trip, and a house they could start their married life in. He had retired from the mission field upon inheriting a large company of trade ships from his father, so he was very wealthy.

I told Tabby that Lief was to come calling on me this evening and asked if she would help me with my hair. She, of course, agreed and giggled about mine being the next wedding. She even let me wear some of her good perfume an aunt had sent her as a birthday gift from Boston.

"Lacy, guess what I heard Mrs. Talbee and Mrs. Mansen talking about?" Tabby asked in a mysterious tone of voice as she hurried into our room.

"What?"

"Not what, but who. Margot!"

"What?" I said quickly.

"I heard they are expelling her from school because she is pregnant and they don't want a whore in their school."

"Wow!" I said, believing it, but still surprised. "Where will she go?" I asked, with a stunned tone.

"I heard the boy who is the father has agreed to marry her and they will live down in the shelter. You know, the broken down one past Elmer Street."

"Who is the father?"

"I think he is some sailor boy that came into port a few months ago," said Dorothy entering the room briskly.

"She is lucky he's going to marry her," Tabby said with some feeling.

"Yes," I said confused, but not very sympathetic. She made a choice, she made a lot of choices. It seems God just caught her on this one. "When is she moving out?" I asked.

"She left early this morning. That's why she wasn't at the wedding!" Dorothy exclaimed.

"Well, I expect they would not have let her into the wedding anyway."

"That's true," Tabby said in agreement with me. Tabby seemed all worked up, but in an excited way. It was big news and something that would be interesting to talk about for days to come when we were bored or nothing else exciting was happening. Tabby moved to the window running her fingers over the carved roses in the window. She still had that fun and capturing smile on her face, like when she had entered the room.

"Oh, look Lacy!" Tabby said excitedly, it's Lief!" She pointed out our window to the sidewalk. Lief was walking straight and tall, he was dressed nice. He had a bouquet of flowers in one hand and the other in his jacket pocket. He was wearing better fitting glasses, ones that were not so big around his eyes. He was so distinguished looking.

Chapter 10

flies

Both Dorothy and Tabby hurried me to the front door, pulling and straightening my dress the whole way down the stairs. By the time we got to the door we were all laughing hysterically. We each took a deep breath and tried not to laugh so boisterously as we opened the door to Lief with flowers! I accepted the flowers, with pleasure, and handed them to Tabby to put in some water.

Then Lief and I set out walking, down the sidewalk and into the city. He offered his arm and I accepted it with nervousness. It was the proper thing to do though.

Today was market day and still this evening there was a swarm of people buying food and such. As we walked along we began to talk. "Lief, tell me about yourself. What do you want to be once you graduate from school?"

"Well, my father wants me to be a doctor or a lawyer, I think I want to continue in the family business though."

"Oh, missionary work?"

"No, that was my mother's passion as a young woman. My father owns a publishing company."

My heart stopped. I stopped. We both turned to look at each other.

"I have been meaning to talk to you about your poetry. I would like to submit some samples of it to my father's editors, if you want me to."

"Yes, that would be wonderful! But I don't want any special treatment," I said with a stern look.

"And you won't get any," he smiled big and I couldn't help but smile back.

We spent the rest of the evening talking about books, authors, the weather when we had nothing else to talk about, and dreams, which was one of my favorite topics. I didn't get to tell anybody my dreams besides Tabby and I only tell her a few of them. Some, I feel, are just too personal and she might not understand.

Lief finally asked me a question I expected to come but wasn't quite sure how to answer. "So, you want to be a writer. Do you ever want to get married?" We continued walking as I thought.

"Yes, of course I want to get married and have a family. But I want to do both, writer and family, not just one." He looked at me as if I were some species he hadn't ever seen before.

"It's good that you want a lot out of your life. But what if you can't find a man who will allow you to be a writer?"

"I would never marry a man who allows me to do anything or does not allow me to do anything. I am not a servant that has to be ruled," I said with a strong, confident voice. The words sounded marvelous together and I was proud of myself.

"I agree," he replied.

I was stunned, how could anyone agree with that, let alone a man. "You do?" I asked in a surprised voice.

"Yes, all people should have fair rights."

Now he just looked at me, like he had before he kissed me at the wedding. My head had all sorts of thoughts going around too fast for me to sort out.

He took my hand and led me behind a brick wall where no one else was. Vines grew all along the wall, and butterflys of majestic colors danced on top of all the glistening flowers. Putting one arm around my waist, he pulled my body gently to his. Time seemed to slow down and it was only him and I, no one else. My words and poems were gone. His other hand was on the back of my neck, one of my auburn curls fell from my messy bun over his fingers. He kissed me. I felt hot from our body heat, and I kissed him back. I never wanted to stop. This felt so safe with his arms all around me, but scary at the same time.

Lief was kissing my neck and my breathing grew deeper, I could feel his lips going up and down. As he massaged my neck with his hand and mouth, the eight o'clock church bell rang. I knew I had to be getting back. Bedtime was in an hour and we were not allowed out past eight p.m. anyway.

"Lief," I said as his lips went back to mine, "I have to go." I tried to get the words in between our long kisses. "The evening bell is ringing."

"Okay," he continued kissing me, then finally let go. I took his arm as we walked back to the school. Smiling at me, he said, "Don't forget to give me some of your poems so I can show my father."

"I won't," I said feeling light and free. He walked me to the front entrance of my school, as I opened the door my hand slid gracefully from his arm.

Chapter 11

by

The next few days passed slowly, I saw Lief every day when he came over to have tea with me and we took a stroll. Tomorrow when he came by I would finally be able to hear what his father thought of my poems. All I could think about though was how he kissed me, so soft, but strong. I wanted to melt every time I thought of him.

Caitlina said once, after I had gotten back from a stroll with him, that I was the luckiest girl in the whole world. I told her not to worry, that her time for love and courting would come soon enough. And with Caitlina's face, it might be sooner than what is proper. She was a true beauty, that one.

My teachers though, were getting frustrated with me for not paying enough attention in class. I would drift off in thoughts, then when they asked me a question I wouldn't know the answer. They would just stand there and shake their heads. Mr. Cambell, especially, was getting agitated and kept saying how important arithmatic was, and if I never learned it how was I supposed to make something of myself. But we both knew that was not true. Women did not make something of themselves, their husbands did. I thought that I was supposed to fall in love and get married. It seems that whatever you do, it is never what anyone wants.

Emma came back from her honeymoon and told us how beautiful the city was and all they did there. It was most delightful to hear. They walked along the beach and went to a big market one day. Most of the time though they spent inside. I hope to visit lots of different cities when I am older. What is the point in hearing about something from another person or book if it's real? Something that is real should not have to be fantisized about.

Then, Dorothy brought up Lief and I. I have always been a rather modest person, I like keeping my personal information to myself. There's nothing wrong with that, except when you live with fifty other girls who are going to grow up and be gossips just like their mothers. It is a never ending cycle.

Dorothy started with, "Lief brought her flowers and gave his arm to her when walking down the main street." She said this with light in her eyes.

I had to defend myself and Lief. "Well, that is the proper thing for a young man to do." I said in almost a yelling tone to my voice.

"Aaa Lacy, I think it is sweet," smiling Emma said. I expected her to understand out of all of them, she is married after all. And she did.

"When are you going to see him again?" Caitlina asked with wide eyes.

Before I answered I looked around the room, there were six of us in all. We each sat straight and proper, perfectly holding our hands in our laps. It was midday and the sun poured through the parlor windows giving the whole room a yellowish, gold tint. The red satin of my chair shone bright and felt like mist as I ran my fingers over it. I cupped my hand around my eyes so I could shield the light and be able to see Caitlina.

"Tonight," I finally answered. "We are going to have late tea, so I best go get ready. Tabby will you help me?" It was more like telling Tabby to help me, than asking, but she understood what I meant. We both scurried out of the room. I had to get out, they were like vulchers, going to pick me apart until there was nothing left. Until the center of my being was like a novel, that everyone knew all its details too.

Once Tabby and I were alone in our room I could tell that she was beaming to ask me a question, so I told her to go ahead. "I wouldn't want you to break your corset seams," I said with a smile.

She laughed, then took a deep breath and said, "Do you love him?"

What is love? I liked spending time with him, and I liked when he kissed me and touched my face. Every time I saw him my stomach fluttered and I just wanted to be near him. Did that all mean I loved him? I came out of my daze and looked in the mirror. There I was, standing with a plain expression on my face and behind me was my best friend smiling so big. What should I say to her when I did not even know what to say to myself? The only response I knew was, "I don't know." It came out along with a release of air, giving the words significant meaning.

Chapter 12

like

"Lacy, my father says he will publish your poetry! But you will have to sign a seven year contract saying you will write for him if your first book sells extremely well. My father thinks you will be the next Emily Dickenson and so do I. What do you think?"

My breath was gone, I couldn't find the air to help me talk. "Your father wants to publish my poetry book?"

"Yes!" Lief answered with a huge grin on his face.

"I, I can't believe this. Oh thank you Lief!" I said, throwing my arms around him.

"You're the one who did all the work," he replied smiling. With my arms still around his neck and our heads resting together, he moved his hands up and down my back, then around my waist. We kissed, and I felt motionless in his arms. He finally let go and moved back to look at me. Touching my cheek, he said in a whispered voice, "I love you."

I still felt empty in some place that should feel full when hearing those words for the first time from a man. I looked into his eyes and felt lost in my brain, it was a maze, and to finish it I needed to know just a little bit more. "Why do you love me?" I asked with a soft, yearning expression.

He touched my hair and said, "Because you are real. You don't try to fit in and be proper, you are who you are. Lacy, I love you because I can be honest with you. You complete me." Tears welled in his eyes.

It was then that I knew how I wanted to feel about him, how I did feel about him. With tears of happiness rolling down my cheeks I whispered back, "I love you too."

Wiping my tears with his hand he hugged me in his strong way. I realized then, as an innocent young woman, that I would get both of my dreams. To be a famous writer and also be a wife and mother.

Lief, I believe, showed me that there are men who want much more from a woman than just pleasure. There are women who can be more than porcelain dolls that are controlled, and that both men and women can have a life that is real. Just real.

That night in my bed, the covers over my body didn't stop a chill through my bones as I lay trying to fall asleep but couldn't. I kept re-playing my time with Lief today, and all the days with him.

I'm in a dream.

I am walking on a dirt and rock path. The little stones go in between my toes, cutting the skin, leaving a trail of blood dots as I continue walking. It is hazy, yet the sky beyond me is blue, the gentlest of blue. Gigantic green leaves hit my side as I keep walking, until I stop. My feet won't let me go any further. I panic. Someone runs by me laughing. I don't see their face and can hardly tell it is a person, except for the laugh.

I start screaming for them to come back and help me. I pull and tug at my legs to be able to walk again. I want to follow that laughing person, see who it is.

"Just stop," I hear a soft, murderous voice say. I look all around, but see no one. I am alone. But there were voices. I am alone. But there was someone running. I am alone. I am alone.

Chapter 13

a

I woke with a start. The sun just came pounding through the windows. I had always thought our rooms to be most plain. There are four beds, two windows, two big dressers which we have to share, then just a full length mirror. No pictures on the walls or any extra do-dads here and there. It was like we lived in a picture. Nothing could be added or changed once it's taken. And we had been taken for a long time.

Looking around to see the other girls still asleep I hurried to get dressed, so hopefully for once I could sit at our dresser without having to move for Tabby. I pulled on my dress and tried to make myself decent when I noticed Rachel waking up, Tabby and Emma also. They stretched their arms and yawned. I finished with my hair and was done. For once I was the one rushing the girls along so we could get down to breakfast!

"So Lacy, how was your late tea?" Tabby asked giggling.

I just rolled my eyes and replied plain and cool, "Fine."

"So, is there going to be a wedding?" asked Rachel.

"How am I supposed to know," I replied. We both told each other we loved one another, but there was no ring.

"Come on Lacy, did he tell you he loved you?" Emma asked, as her eyes increased in size with each of my answers.

I stumbled on my words, like I usually did when I was nervous. "Ye-yes," I blushed, tried not to, but did.

"Aaaaa!" The three of them screamed happily.

"Good Lord, there is going to be a wedding," Emma said in a Southern mocking tone.

"So, has he given you a ring yet?" Tabby pushed.

"No, so I do not want to hear anything about it outside of this room. That is just what I need, to scare Lief and embarrass him."

"We promise we won't say a word," Emma smiled and the other girls nodded their heads.

I looked around at each of them in a serious face, then burst out laughing. "He told me he loves me!" I said with a big smile on my face, giving a little hop of joy. They all lept off their beds and gave me wild, smiling friends forever hugs.

That's when we heard loud knocking on our wall from Dorothy's room, right next to ours. They were complaining about us making too much noise. We all laughed and quieted down, but before Tabby got dressed she gave me a big hug. Her smile was so sweet, and I felt so happy.

Chapter 14

page

"So, Miss Slucipher, I trust your stroll with Mr. Phelpsson was delightful," said Mrs. Talbee as she passed by our breafeast table.

"Yes it was, thank you," I responded. She gave a smile then continued down the table rows. Mrs. Talbee really was an interesting woman. She seemed to know everything about everyone in this entire building. It was like she could see all of us everywhere we went. Mrs. Talbee was a rather tall woman and very slender. She had graying hair, and always wore it back in a very tight bun. It was so tight that it looked like it would hurt her head to have all her hair pulling her skin like that. She walked fast and proud, looking at each of the girls along the tables before sitting down to her place at the head of the staff table. She seemed to do everything perfect. Didn't that drive her insane, ever?

Breakfast was good, eggs, pancakes, sausage and orange juice. Emma and Tabby kept eyeing me from their seats at the table, throwing all of us into laughter. I'm sure the other girls thought us crazy, and some were still mad that we had been making enough noise to wake them. They would have had to get up soon anyway.

By late afternoon I was stressed from classes and tired of keeping the secret of my poems being published. As I sat in the wooden school desk, trying to take in all my teacher was saying, my mind would go back and forth. From lessons to daydreams, it was all I could do to keep myself focused. I tapped my pencil on my desk trying to keep myself alert, until the teacher scolded me for making unnecessary noise. If she only knew. Really! When would the bell ring, I thought, trying to keep an eye on the teacher, but on the clock too.

After class it was social time, when we could do basically anything we wanted. I knew exactly what I wanted to do. I walked by Tabby and gave her a note to meet me in the courtyard, right now!

I was already standing by the fountain when she came out. She had a confused look on her face, so I smiled to let her know everything was okay.

"Tabby, walk with me, will you? I need to tell you some news I have!" Her eyes glowed with delight and she looped arms with me and waited for me to spill.

"Lief's father owns a publishing company, and so Lief showed some of my poetry to him, and he wants to publish it! My own poetry book!" I smiled from corner to corner. She smiled and gave me a little hug.

"Oh Lacy, this is what you have always wanted. I am so happy for you!"

"But please do not tell anyone, not even Emma or Rachel. Just not yet."

"I promise," she said with a childs happiness. We continued walking arm in arm through the hot sun until Tabby turned and spoke, "Lacy, I think I am going to leave."

"What?" I said, fast, quick, sharp. "What do you mean you are going to leave?"

"Dorothy's parents are paying for us to travel to England after graduation. My parents certainly don't care what I do, and besides it would be a good place to find a husband. The ship will leave in two weeks time."

Cold tears ran down from my eyes, they met with my sun warmed cheeks. I was surprised my face didn't start sizzling. "But Tabby, what about me? I will never see you again."

She shrugged her shoulders, not being able to talk. I didn't understand and was confused. I started yelling hysterically, "You are going all that way just to find a man? Some stupid man to break your heart and leave you dying inside? Tabby, you can find a husband here." I was crying and couldn't say anymore.

Tabby had both of her hands over her face, just sobbing. I had never seen her so upset before. I closed my eyes that burned from the tears, saw images of her fixing my hair and giggling when we raced down the stairs to meet Lief. They filled my memory. She was my best friend, my best friend who was going to leave.

Chapter 15

that's

I hadn't said or looked at Tabby for the past week, I couldn't. When I did I saw her image on a grand ship, leaving me, waving goodbye. I couldn't deal with that.

Poor Lief though, had to deal with all my frustration regarding Tabby. It became a routine. He would come to tea, then we would take a walk, then I would express my anguish verbally. I had to tell someone about our fight and he was the one I wanted to tell it to. After I'd finished telling him the whole story over and over again, he would start kissing me and hugging me. That always made everything fine again, until the next day when everything started over again. But I had come to believe that I kept telling him how upset I was over Tabby traveling to England, me wanting her to stay, and getting all upset over it so he would kiss me like it was our last kiss. Sneaky I am, but I truly didn't want Tabby to leave. She was like my sister.

The days seemed to be going by more slowly. Day after day I would do the same thing, and it was driving me to have a very short temper, even with Caitlina. I just felt so lost. Also, the weather had changed, it was hot, grayish out and the haze came in earlier than it used to. I felt sick most of the time and just wanted to stay in my bed and hide under my covers. But could not fall asleep, tried and never fell asleep. I lay stiff in my bed as the bright moon shone through the window. It seemed so lonely up there, all alone, like God forgot to give it a companion. Maybe that's what the stars are for.

My mind came alive with thoughts of life. What was it that I wanted to do? Did I want to get married, live in a town house and be a writer? Or sail the seas, travel through different times where I'd never been. Dear God, why did I feel a sense of jealousy? I loved Lief, I did. If I were to leave, to travel, would I miss the chance of publishing my book? Would I lose the life I was used to? Would I lose Lief? I couldn't bear that. What should I do? My head was swarming and it frightened me. I felt out of control within myself.

I had my aunt's money, which would last a while if I traveled. Why couldn't people turn off their brains, so they didn't have to think? So much of the time I wished I could pause life and just step out of it. Like stepping off a boat when the rocking has stopped. It would be like you're in a different zone. One that is better? I'm not sure.

I'm in a dream.

I have a light green flowing dress on and my hair is rippling up and down my back with rich auburn color as I walk. Like church bells being rung. I'm walking through the beautiful jungle of Africa. Leaves the size of elephants feet brush soft along my side as I walk barefoot on the warm heated sand of a trail I hadn't noticed before. There's a baby monkey swinging in the tree above me, it has a sweet face and round cheeks filled with bananas. His tail looks about a foot long and he is the color of ginger.

I hear my name softly being called. I look all around me, but see no one. I am scared and start to run towards the voice, I answer back, but no change. I run faster and faster, my dress sweeping past all the leaves, until time seems to slow down. I reach a clearing and step into it. I turn in a circle to see who was calling me. As I turn I feel my body getting heavier and my legs can no longer support myself. I collapse to my knees on the ground, breathe heavily. I can hear it. I see my mother's open locket lying on the ground, pick it up and look to my side. I see a young man running from me, he's laughing as he runs to where the jungle starts again. I call to him to stop, and he does. He turns around and smiles at me. It is my father. Not the father I remember though, it's when he was younger. I call to him to stop, wait for me, I don't want to stay here by myself. He backs with a stumble as I come closer. He speaks. "No." I don't understand and try to ask, but he is gone, and so is the locket that was in my hand. And so am I.

Chapter 16

turned

"Lacy, wake up, you're having a nightmare," Tabby said shaking me.

"What?"

"You were screaming, what did you dream about?" Her face was panicked.

I had forgotten I was upset with her, "I, I don't know." I knew, but just didn't want to talk about it.

She blew out a loud release of air, then said, "Well, you better get dressed, it's Saturday and Lief is calling on you this morning, remember?"

"Oh yes, I had forgotten. Thanks." I wasn't sure how things were between us. Sometimes it seemed when people got in fights it was forgotten in the next few days. Or they made it that way. She nodded her head, gave a slight smile, then left the room.

I was alone, just like at the ending and beginning of my dream. What was that dream I'd had? Was it just a nightmare or did it mean something? Lately I had been having dreams that made no sense and kept me scared at night to close my eyes. I was afraid sometimes that my dreams wouldn't let me wake up again. Had I just been lucky in all of my past dreams, lucky that I am still here?

I quickly got dressed and ready to meet Lief. He was waiting in the parlor when I came down to greet him. He gave me a beautiful smile and escorted me out of the school for a stroll down the sidewalk. I felt nervous and not sure what to say. I really couldn't get my mind off the dream I'd had. It was a mystery to me about what it meant.

I think Lief could tell that something was bothering me, because he then asked, "Did you sleep well?"

"Oh, yes, you.?"

"Yes," he smiled and turned to look at me. "Lacy, I want to ask you a question."

I gulped, "Yes?"

He took both my hands, looked at me in the eyes and started, "You know how I feel about you, don't you?"

"Of course I do," I said with a mellowed smile.

"I love you and I, I," he paused and sweat started on his forehead. He got down on one knee and my heart quickened as he asked, "Will you marry me?"

I loved Lief, and if it hadn't been for that dream I would of said yes in a second. "Lief, remember when you asked me if I had slept well?"

"Yes," he looked confused, as I would be too if I were him.

"Well, I had a dream." He got up from his knee and stood in front of me while I told him my entire dream. Then I explained to him how I'd had other dreams that were similar, involving my parents and Africa. But that this was the first dream where I actually saw my parents faces clearly. It had to mean something. When I finished, he didn't say anything, just stared at me.

He took a breath and asked, "What are you saying?"

"I am saying that maybe I should go to Africa. Try to find out more information about how my parents died. Just try to find some answers." Tears started slightly falling down my cheeks. "But I still love you, I don't want to lose you. I love you," I said with shortened breath.

He gave me a strong hug. "You will never lose me," he whispered in my ear. Then he slipped a ring on my wedding finger and kissed my hand. "When you are done looking for answers, you will come back to me?" He touched my cheek as he spoke.

"I promise." Our foreheads rested against each other, then I turned to go, but stopped to say something more. "I love you Lief, it will not be long until we are together again."

He smiled and came to kiss me one last time. "I will see you in my dreams," he said, then walked away.

I watched him as he turned the corner, then looked down at the gold band on my finger, it had a sapphire on it. It was very shiny, brand new from the jeweller. It was mine alone, not a hand-me-down, but only for my finger intended. I took it off to look at all its profiles, when I noticed something engraved in the band, "*To my love, return to me whenever away.*" A tear fell, and I slipped the ring back on my left hand. Had I just ruined everything? Would there be no getting him back?

My Great Aunt once told me that, "a man's heart is one of the most fragile things in this world, do not play around with it like some do." She seldom said things that seemed of much importance, but this had always stayed in the back of my mind.

I walked back to the school and found Tabby in our room, packing her suitcase for England.

"I'm sorry," I said quietly. She turned around and gave me a hug. We stood there on the wood floor, hugging for what seemed like hours. When we let go, I showed her my ring. "We are going to get married," I paused, "but I have something to do first."

I went to Africa for a reason that was real to me, something I couldn't put away and hide from myself. I went to Africa to find out who I was, who I am, and who I will become.

Selected Poems
of
Lacy Slucipher

She looked at me as if I were nothing.
She looked at me as if I were everything.
She looked at me just to see me.

I wish I could run in the wind
and be swept away,
fly through the clouds
and meet no one
except thee.

I drift off in class,
I think about a poem
then laugh,
I get lost in my dreams
and imagination,
I feel free to be
who I know
no one can see,
I fantasize and wonder
when I know I should
be asleep slumber.

The crickets sound loud
through the night
The moon shines bright
as if it had something to fight
They sing together to mark the night

Prince Charming is dead,
I heard,
he said.
He was found on the ground
with no girl
all around.
Prince Charming is dead
oh well beauty has fled.

Beauty and poise
wrapped around,
silenced in a noise,
feelings and touch
left alone with nothing much,
sadness and anger
something different and stranger.

I sit plain and straight
Can't flich or start a fight
Thin and proper is my name
Tuck me away until needed
Obey the rules and don't skip school
You are wrong and they are right
Deal with it
It's your life.

I feel seperate from all the rest
Like I'm in some other place
I'm just here to fill a space
No one seems to notice
No one seems to have any grace
I am all alone
Somewhere different than this place

Hi
hello
how are you
do you even care
if I were to sit here and stare
so I'll waste the day
there's plenty more anyway
so I'll just sit here
don't mind me
quiet as a mouse can be
oh well one loss of a day
to add to the tree.

Part Two

Saldanha, Africa

"You can't have a future without a past"

Chapter 17

Poems

I sailed the seas for five months. As the days went by I realized that I had turned sixteen without knowing it. One has to work hard at keeping track of the days when one is at sea. Things seem to go slower and you forget about the life you were once so used to.

Christmas came and went. The air was mildly warm even though it usually is snowing back home during the Christmas holiday. It didn't feel like Christmas at all. The sailors certainly didn't tone their language down for the holy day either, and the holiday dinner wasn't much. I think they even tried to pass some tropical fish off as a turkey. That really made me sick.

Back at school I can still remember the smells of ham and turkey roasting, dozens and dozens of pies baking in the ovens, and filling the school with the smells. The grand entrance to our school was always so beautifully decorated. A huge tree with beautiful ornaments all over it would be set up. The staircase would have real garlands lined all the way up to the branching off of the hallways. Some of the girls would go home for the holidays, and others like me would stay, and eat the best food ever. Tabby and I would stay up all night talking about how we would go and play wildly in the fresh new snow that would sweep in that night. It was so magical and it truly was heaven on earth.

Everyone was always in a good mood, I think that was the hardest time of the whole year to pay attention in class. Wondering if you would get a Christmas greeting from that special someone you admired, hoping that you might. Of course, up until this year I had never had a sweetheart, then the first Christmas to come along with Lief and I together, I am gone. Thousands of miles away from him.

I was able to graduate a year early, so when I returned from this journey I wouldn't have to attend school anymore. Even though my grades were poor, I had mastered the main things; sewing, cooking, setting a table correctly, and starting a conversation when awkward silence fell. To my teachers that's all a young lady really needs to know.

My journey was by cargo ship, so there weren't many other people to socialize with while traveling. Except the sailors, but they were crude and made unseemly gestures as I strolled past them. The Captain, Jack Follow, I hardly ever saw. Maybe once, but that was only when he was on the deck smoking what was rumored to be opium. I had heard it was one of the main things bought and sold in South Africa. I think it is supposed to make one happy, I wouldn't know. I heard that one of the reasons Captain stays in his cabin was because he had lost his love, but never got over it. She was a black woman who he had captured for slavery, but then fell in love with. She was shot though, through the head. It was illegal to bring slaves over, and in all the hustle and bustle between the crewmen and the United States government officials someone shot her. I think it was Captain himself, but nobody knows and nobody hardly talks about it. It happened quite some years ago.

Also on the ship were a group of two missionary families, eleven people in all. The Calloway's and Sower's. We talked now and then, and I asked them if they had known my parents. They hadn't and seemed eager to change the subject. Both Mrs. Calloway and Mrs. Sower turned white at the mere mention of my parents names, and then scurried away. I don't know why.

The ship rocked, a never ending sway back and forth. It got to the point that I felt I was losing my mind, along with everyone else. One day as I was sick over the side of the ship, one of the crewmen came over and grabbed me. He pulled my waist against his body and held me there tight, as I screamed and kicked. He just whispered, "I won't hurt you if you just come with me for a while." He smelled like whiskey and no shower in months. At that moment Mr. Calloway came and physically pulled the man away. Watching him crash to the ground I ran to my cabin below deck and stayed there the remainder of the trip, with the exception of being sick over the railing each day. The best time to find out if you are seasick is not when going on the sea for five months.

When we docked in Saldanha, I didn't know what month it was. I wasn't even sure of the year, five months seemed more like five years. I felt older than when this journey to find my parents had first begun. I felt like I was a thirty five year old woman, my skin tight against my face. Probably from the sea salt and sun.

I walked down the plank, tripping on my own feet while carrying the three suitcases of my belongings that I had brought on this God forsaken trip. I stumbled to a carriage where an African loaded my luggage and asked my destination. I told him to the nearest hotel. Where else would I be going when not even knowing a living soul?

As we made our way through town, dust got in my eyes from the wagons in front of us. It made my eyes swollen, so it looked like I had just been crying. I guess it really didn't matter, I mean, who here did I have to impress?

My bags were loaded off the wagon and left on the hotel steps. Soon, a gray haired, hunched over woman helped me carry my bags up a long, hot flight of stairs to a mosquito filled room. Thanking her as she turned to go, I noticed that she was as wide as she was tall! Tossing my bags onto the bed I watched as the bed sank nearly to the floor from their weight. Really pathetic if you ask me.

I walked over to my window and viewed the city from three flights up. The Calloway's and Sower's were driving off into the rain forest. That, I expect, is where the rest of the missionaries live. I shall have to go out there some time later. Maybe it would be cooler out there. Here, where I am, it is dust and heat. That's all, except of course, the sea.

I hadn't noticed until now how the population here was African. Everywhere. People as dark as the chocolate that was served every Sunday at school by

Mrs. Talbee. Some of them were driving carriages to and fro like my driver. Some were by the seashore sorting the daily catch of fish, others selling baskets they had made. It was a population of one kind. A kind I felt I wouldn't be able to fit into. Or couldn't fit into.

Children ran barefoot along side the road, barely dressed. I felt the proper thing to do was to shield my eyes from them. What would my teachers think of me seeing half naked boys? It must be different here though, all people have skin, and so it doesn't matter if it shows or not.

Chapter 18

twist

I swatted at the bugs as I came through a swarm of them. How could people live like this, like animals? There was a bug on my arm at that moment, I could tell it was ready to eat me alive. This was the moment to show who is the boss in the animal kingdom. I steadied my hand in a raised position, counted to five and...smack! It was dead and I won!

My mind was racing with thoughts of what I should do first. I had no idea who to talk to or what to say. And I didn't want people, everytime I mentioned my parents very name, to run away from me like Mrs. Calloway and Mrs. Sower's had. Why, what did my parents do?

Unpacking all my things had been quite a big job. Deciding where to put this and that, scared that it might get stolen, or ruined by all the bloody bugs. What would I do if Great Aunt Selma's money was lost? I would be stuck here forever with no one. Alone in a world. But then again, there was my Lief, he would come for me. Then things wouldn't be so bad. I promised him before leaving that I would write the minute I arrived, that I was safe. I best get to that.

May 2, 1909 – Thursday

Dearest Lief,

I have arrived here safely, one week ago today, so please try and not worry about me too much. I am getting settled into the hotel and plan on starting my journey to find my parents tomorrow.

It is very hot in Saldanha, South Africa. There are many bugs, everywhere, even in my bedroom. It is quite gross. But I guess there is really nothing I can do about it.

The trip over here was very long. The seas were not too wild, but I was quite seasick the whole time. I made some acquaintances aboard ship. Last names are Calloway and Sower. I was glad they were there, so I would not be alone with just the sailors.

Dear, I miss you so much. I think of you every minute and wish so much to be back with you right now. Once, on the ship, I thought I saw you and ran towards you, but it was not you, just some sailor. Thank you for understanding that I have to do this. I promise that I will not be gone too long. Then, we can get married like we planned to do after I get back.

I see you every night in my dreams. I love you.

Yours Forever,

Lacy

The next morning I awoke with a start. There were thousands of bugs crawling all over my face. On my eyes and the corners of my mouth. I sat up and banged my head around in the air trying to get the bugs off. I felt like a mad woman, throwing a fit in her room. I think I even scared myself.

I calmed down some after most of the bugs were off. Just then there was a light knock on my door. I opened it to the hotel maid who was wheeling in a wash stand with a basin and pitcher of water. After the maid excused herself and left, I used the wash cloth and warm water. Rinsing and wringing out the cloth time and time again, cleaning myself, trying to make sure I was as clean as I could get. I put on one of my dresses and headed down the humid stairway to where breakfast was being served.

"Dear, you may sit there, by Mr. and Mrs. Tanna," said an older, thin, white woman. I assumed she was the wife to the owner of this hotel.

"Thank you," I replied. I sat down on a cloth covered chair. The cloth was colored rich golds, reds and blues all swirled together. It was a beautiful print, very wild from what I was used to, I think that's why I liked it so much. I sat down at a round, wooden dining table. It seated fifteen people around it, kind of like the tables back at school.

"So dear, you look very young to be so far from home," said Mrs. Tanna

"Yes, thank you."

"What is your name honey?" said another woman across from me.

"Lacy Slucipher, ma'am."

Everyone turned to look at me. The room grew as silent and still as a graveyard.

Mr. Tanna spoke meekly, "Slucipher, you say?"

"Yes, that is right. May I ask why you question me?" Both Mr. and Mrs. Tanna gulped. I didn't know what to think.

Mrs. Tanna began, "Just making sure we heard you right, that is all dear."

I was not sure that was all. The fact that the whole table stopped to look at me when I said my name told me differently. I finished my porriage, then went back up to my room to get my umbrella and money purse. Today was the day I wanted to find some answers.

Chapter 19

and

The dust kicked up under my feet and the sun beat down on me like a thousand wool blankets being thrown on me over and over again. My face itched with numerous bug bites and I felt sweaty and sticky all over. Miserable was the only word that was in my vocabulary at that moment.

"Get your past and future told here folks," announced a wrinkled, old African man. Behind him was a colorful curtain hanging with a sign that read, *"Let Madamlee tell your future and past - only 5 cents American"*

Even though this all sounded like a bunch of malarky, I thought I might as well try it, what did I have to lose? Except my five cents.

"Okay, I would like to get my future told, please. Here is five cents," I said.

"Good, right this way Miss." The man led me behind the curtain to a small wooden table with a glass ball on it. I sat down in the chair, regretting that I had gotten myself into this, and scared. These people could be insane, escaped convicts, oh well.

"Aaaa, I thought I would be seeing you here," said a black woman dressed up in gold bracelets, earrings and a beautiful bright cloth wrapped around her as a dress. She was majestic looking and stole all my other thoughts.

She sat down across the table and stared at me for awhile, then spoke, "Lacy, what would you like *Madamlee* to show you in the crystal ball? Your love that will come, if he will be rich or not?"

"Well, I want to know what happened to my parents," I replied, shaken to realize that she knew my name.

"Your parents?"

"Yes."

She didn't say anything more, just tapped her fingers on the table. Then said, "I shall try, but I want you to know that one of my most difficult tasks is trying to contact the dead. They never seem too open to talk about their past life on earth, but I will try."

My eyes must have been open a mile wide, watching everything she did. She started off with a wicked sounding phrase, "sssssacka ddddddoenaaaa, criiiiiiieeeeeessss." Then performed a weird motion with her hands, waving them up and down through the air, letting them just dangle as if they were light as feathers. She lightly rested them on the crystal ball, moving her hands all over it.

I could hear myself breathing and felt sweat trickle down my forehead. Everything was silent. *Madamlee's* hands were just resting on the crystal ball, and she was in a daze. I wasn't sure what to do, had she fallen asleep? I was about to say something when she spoke up.

"Lacy, I cannot, there is nothing more."

"What?" I asked rather loudly.

"This is a task that I cannot just tell you the answer to. You must find out what exactly happened to your parents by yourself. I am sorry."

Feeling like my dreams had been smashed, I knew I shouldn't have ever come in here. I was mad and confused. "So, do you know what happened to my parents though?" I choked out.

"Yes, but I cannot tell you. There was a promise made that you have to find it out on your own."

Swallowing back tears I asked, "Well, what do I do now then?"

"Find the truth," was her simple reply.

Find the truth, find the truth! She was supposed to be my truth, my mind told me over and over. "Maybe I will go out to the missionary camp, perhaps someone can help me there," I said, implying that she hadn't helped me at all.

She gave a slight smile, "You do that."

I walked out of her little secluded place and back onto the main street. Not knowing how far out in the forest the missionary camp was, I decided to hire a buggy to take me there. "Excuse me," I said to a young negro man. "Will you take me to the missionary camp outside of town?"

"Yes, ma'am."

"Thank you." He helped me into the buggy and we started out of town. It probably took fifteen minutes to get there, so I was glad I hadn't tried to walk in the sweltering heat.

Along the way I noticed how the trees of the forest were just beautiful, lush green leaves as big as a small child. It was amazing. Also, the colorful birds, every color you could possibly think of. There were monkeys swinging in the trees too. When the carriage went by they would just be still, like they had suddenly been turned to ice. The monkeys looked similar to the one from my dream a while back. I didn't see any snakes and was glad too.

Chapter 20

turn

We arrived at the missionary camp. There were tents set up, and a couple of log houses. There were white children running around and the women were doing laundry. I saw a few men reading the Bible, the rest of the men must be in other villages preaching. I saw Mrs. Calloway from a distance and waved. She waved back and gave a small smile, then hurried back into her tent. I felt out of place, but my driver must have felt more so. He was the only black person in the entire camp.

"Ma'am, would you like me to wait for you," my driver asked with a pleasant smile.

"Yes, thank you, and what is your name?"

"Zachin, ma'am."

"Well, thank you Zachin, I am Lacy Slucipher."

"Slucipher. You wouldn't be related to…, never mind, I'll just wait here for you." He gave me a long glance.

"Thank you," I said slowly, with a sense of curiosity. I walked over to where most of the women were working, or sitting and sewing.

"Excuse me, my name is Lacy Slucipher, and I am trying to find out what happened to my parents. They died some time ago, but, did any of you know them?"

They all shook their heads and continued with their tasks, except they did them a lot faster.

I gave a sigh, and made sure they all heard it, then turned around and ran into a small child.

"Oh, sorry honey," I apologized and tried to walk on, but the girl ran after me.

"You are Miss Slucipher," the girl asked.

"Yes!" That sure got my attention.

"I know where your parents are." She held out a dirty hand, but I took it anyway. She led me up a path of dirt, out of site from camp. We passed a small pond on the way. Then we came to a place that took my breath away. It was shielded with huge elephant leaves, tropical birds sat on top like guards. The small girl pushed through the leaves and led me into a circular place that was totally surrounded with green leaves. There, in the middle of the circle, were two tomb stones that read:

Jenny Slucipher   *Carl Slucipher*

Nothing more than that, no dates or phrases. Like they were just some people that had died and been thrown away. It brought tears to my eyes and I fell to my knees. I didn't understand any of it.

"What did this mean? I knew they were dead, but why were they buried way out here?" I was sobbing and couldn't control it.

"Maggie," a woman's voice yelled.

The little girl started to run back, "That's my mama."

"Wait, tell me please, why were they buried way out here?" I could barely talk.

The little girl stopped running and stood there looking at me from a ways off, then spoke lightly, almost in a whisper, "Because they were shunned." Then she ran off, swatting at the leaves on her way back to camp.

I didn't understand why they were shunned. I was only getting bits and pieces, how was I supposed to know what to do.

"Miss Slucipher, Miss Slucipher," a man's voice was yelling.

"Yes," I answered through tears. "I am over here," my voice quivered.

It was Zachin. "We should be heading back, it will get dark soon," he paused, "are you alright, ma'am?"

I wiped tears from my flushed cheeks and held out my hand. "Help me up," I whispered.

"But, ma'am, you don't have gloves on. If anyone saw I could get in trouble, be killed for touching you," he said, trembling.

"Damn everyone! Please, help me up," I kind of yelled. My words came out one at a time and in gasps from crying.

The ride back to town felt much longer than the ride out there. We were silent the whole time, but it was a different sort of silence than before.

"Tomorrow if you need to go anywhere, I'll be right where I was today, and will take you wherever you want to go," Zachin said in his kind way.

"Thank you Zachin," I said with more than just thanks for the ride, but also with being there for me.

It was nearly dark once we arrived back at the hotel. I was very tired and felt like sleeping for the rest of my life. Before going up to my room, I had tea with Mrs. Gahdakly. She was the lady who I had assumed was the owners wife, and in which I was right.

"Dear, sit down, it looks like you have had a hard day. Here, have some tea, it is a special kind of tea that they only make and sell over here. It will let you rest well."

"Thank you, Mrs. Gahdakly." Taking a drink of the strong tea, I quickly sat it back down.

"Please, call me Pag," she said smiling, and I was glad that she had said that. "Why exactly are you here, dear?"

"I am here to find out what the big mystery is about my parents?

"Aaa, Jenny and Carl."

When I heard her say that I nearly choked on my own tongue. "You knew them," I exclaimed rather loudly.

"Yes, of course. Fine, fine people. Like you."

I smiled at her compliment, but needed more. "Did you know them very well? How did you know them? Why when I say my last name does everyone get quiet?"

I was now leaning forward in my chair, so into the moment that I did not realize I was being improper. I don't think Pag much cared though.

"I will tell you all that I know. But you best get comfortable, it is long." She made herself comfortable in her chair, then began what I had, for so long, waited to hear.

Chapter 21

to

"It was over sixteen years ago that this happened. Your mother, Jenny Hugga, wasn't much older than you are now when she had decided to sail to South Africa with another family to become a missionary. She sailed here with my husband, myself and our four children. Jenny, what a sweet girl she was, so polite and charming to be around. She reminds me so much of you Lacy."

I couldn't help but let a tear out, then Pag continued, "We, as you know on your ship ride over here, spent five months sailing to get here. Jenny loved the sea and all the sailors on board had a huge crush on her. She was so beautiful, with fiery auburn hair, much like yours. Well, one evening at dinner she was seated by the Captain himself, which was a great honor."

….. *"Miss Hugga, I trust your voyage across the Atlantic Ocean is an enjoyable one?"*

"Yes, thank you Captain." Jenny looked down at her plate and blushed.

"Please call me Jack," the Captain replied while never taking his eyes off of her.….

"Wait," I interrupted Pag's memories. "That wouldn't be Captain Jack Follow, would it?"

"Yes, dear, why?"

"He was my Captain on the way over here."

"Was he know," Pag said, looking up from her tea with a surprised expression on her face.

"Yes," I said, feeling confused.

Then Pag began again, "The Captain had a beautiful smile. He was a very handsome man and young to be a captain at only thirty. I could tell from that one dinner that they were taken with each other. While everyone else socialized amongst themselves, those two kept to just one another. He would say something funny that would make her laugh. Jenny was always laughing. I didn't know Jack that well, but everyone who has known him says that he is a very serious man. Not around Jenny though. She is the only one that brought out his joy for life. She was his life.

You could see them taking walks along the deck and standing on the balcony rail looking down deep into the ocean, whispering things into each others ears. They were always together, everyone aboard the ship could see that those two were in love.

I though, was scared for Jenny. A sailors life is a hard one. If they were to get married she would always be away from him when he was out on the raging sea, doing God knows what."

Chapter 22

make

"That's when I took Jenny aside and talked to her," Pag continued.

…..*"Jenny, dear, I love you like you were my own, and I do not want you to get hurt."*

"Pag, Jack is a gentleman, how could you suggest that I should leave him?"

"I just want you to be careful, you yourself have heard of nasty tales of women who give themselves up to seafaring men."

"He's not like that Pag, how dare you say such things."…..

"By that time Jenny was very upset and crying. She ran out of the room and down the hall. I felt terrible and wasn't sure what I should do. I loved Jenny so much, and I didn't want this sea captain who was twenty some years older than her to take advantage of her.

I decided that I would try talking to her the next morning. Maybe if she slept on what I had said to her she would have time to calm down, me too for that matter. But other things happened.

Like I said, Jenny took off running down the hall, she was running and crying all at the same time. She was mad, confused and didn't know what to do. So she went to Jack. He was sleeping in his cabin at the time, since it was late at night. Jenny pounded loud at his door, when he opened it she ran inside and shut it tight behind her. She was soaked from the rain that had been pouring down that whole day, and she was still very upset from all I had said to her," Pag paused.

"Lacy dear, I think you know what happened once she was inside his cabin. Your mother was young, scared, mad and confused. And here was a man that had seen the world, and seemed to your mother to have all the answers. Your mother was in love with Jack and he with her, and so that made you."

"No," I started to cry, "how could she do such a bad thing?"

Pag hugged me and asked if she should continue or not. I knew she must, I had to know the whole truth, though it was breaking my heart. To think my own mother did what she did before she was married. Just like Margot did, who was banned from school because of it.

Pag cleared her throat and took another sip of tea before starting up again. "The next morning Jenny came to me and told me what she had done. She and I were both crying, and swore to each other not to tell anyone. But we both had to watch out for signs of pregnancy.

Well the signs came. We knew for certain that she was in the very early stages of pregnancy. We would reach land in only a weeks time, so she and Jack planned on getting married right away. They had to, or else your mother would be disowned by everyone who knew her, her life would be ruined.

When we landed, your mother and Jack quickly found someone that would marry them in two weeks time. But the day their wedding was to take place, your mother found a letter hidden away in Jack's suitcase." "It read,

…..Dearest Jack,

I miss you so much. I have already waited five months as you traveled down to South Africa, I guess I can wait five more for your return. There is wonderful news! We are to have a baby! He or she will be born before your ship docks here again. My wish is that you could be home for the birth. I wish it even though it is not proper for a husband to be present when his wife is giving birth. We both know we don't follow the rules, so for the life of me I don't know why our last name is Follow.

Write back as soon as you can my dear, I love you.

Love NaeLa…..

"The letter was waiting for Jack at the Post Office when our ship docked, and he had hidden it away without saying a word to Jenny. Your mother was very upset, she came to me and asked what she should do. I didn't know at all how to advise her on that, except that she needed to talk to Jack and find out why he lied to her. And so she did."

…..*"Jack, who is NaeLa and what is this?"* *Jenny asked, showing Jack the letter she had found. Jack sat down on his bed and read the letter again and again, not saying anything. "Well," Jenny yelled with tears streaming down her face.*

"NaeLa is my wife, she is a negro, but I feel in love with her. Now she is pregnant with our child." Jack stared at Jenny as she slowly fell to the bedside, rocking back and forth, crying.

"How could you? I thought you loved me," Jenny was sobbing and shaking.

"I do love you," Jack whispered as he tried to stroke Jenny's hair.

"No! No, do not tell me that! You have a whole other family!" Now Jenny was yelling and crying hysterically. She took off the wedding band and threw it at Jack, leaving him just two hours before they would have wed.

Jack came after Jenny who was running down the dirt road in her bare feet. Her hair fell to a mess as she was running and she could hear Jack yelling for her, "Stop, please I never meant…," Jack was crying now and out of breath.

Jenny kept on running and that was the last time she ever heard of or saw Jack Follow…..

"Jenny ran all the way here to this hotel, which my husband had just bought for us to live in. In a weeks time Jenny had met a young man and married him. His name was Carl Slucipher, he was a young missionary in the village. She told him, before they married, that she was pregnant. But he already knew, everyone knew. Nothing can be kept secret in a small town, like this one was back then. And everyone was very cruel to your mother and to Carl, your father, for marrying a woman who was not pure. But your father loved your mother, and that did not matter at all to him."

Chapter 23

a

"So, my true father is Captain Jack Follow?" I asked in disbelief.

"That's right sweetheart," Pag replied tenderly.

"I feel like I don't belong anywhere anymore. I don't know what to think."

"Your mother loved you very much, and so did your father. And Jack, he loved your mother more than anything. But it just could not have worked with him."

"Please tell me the rest," I urged Pag.

"Well, Jack left the following week. He sailed back to New York Harbor where he joined NaeLa and their baby son. But, bad things happened. People began to notice and talk about this unusual couple with their child. Rumors started and word got out that someone had captured a slave girl and then slept with her. Everything got crazy. Jack and NaeLa took their child and tried to escape back to South Africa were NaeLa was originally from, but they didn't get that far.

There was so much confusion, everyone was yelling, the government officials were shouting and everyone was running. Somehow NaeLa got shot in the head. Many say that Jack accidently shot her. Others say a government official shot her, but nobody knows for sure. But, their baby was still safe. When the officials first came aboard the ship NaeLa had hidden her baby in an old storage place. It was used for hiding rum in, so if pirates attacked the ship the sailors wouldn't be without their blessed rum.

In a few days, after the commotion died down, Jack took his son and continued sailing back to South Africa. Once there, he gave his baby to a local family to take care of and raise. He knew a black boy would only have a good life if he was with his own kind. He did that for his son.

After that, Jack never tried to look for his son, but stayed with his ship and tried to stay away from people too. His heart was broken, from the loss of his wife and son. But also for his Jenny, which I believe he still looks for when he docks his ship every year."

"Pag, so does that mean I have a half brother, who is black?" I asked, my mind racing and confused.

"Yes, it does."

"Well, I have got to find him. He, he has to still be here. Do you know where he lives?" Now I had a new goal that I must conquer, and that was to find my brother.

"I do not know anything about your half brother, even what town he is in. But I believe originally he was left with people from nearby."

"Tomorrow I am going to look for him. But I am still confused about something. Why was all this information always kept from me? My Great Aunt Selma must have known about this, but no one ever told me."

"Yes, your aunt did know. She was very upset with Jenny for becoming pregnant before she was married. Your mother and aunt never got along very well after that. Jenny told me once that she and her aunt were always very close, but after the scandal her aunt wanted nothing to do with her anymore. A lot of people, including those at the missionary camp felt the same way."

"Oh, that is why my parents were buried so far out there," I said, feeling like this mystery was beginning to make some sense.

"Yes, the other missionary families stopped talking to Jenny and Carl. Jenny's aunt only ever saw her once right after the baby was born, you Lacy. And then, as you know, they saw each other just a few times before your parents deaths. She tried hard to hate you as well, but there was always a part of your great aunt that was open to you. You were the reason she talked to your mother at all."

The room was very dark, except for the lamps that were lit, and I could only see the outline of Pag's face. I had finally found the truth. My biological father was Captain Jack Follows and I also had a half brother that is an African. But where was he? When I was on the ship coming over here, did Jack, the Captain know it was me? And what about my parents death?

"Pag, what about my parents death?"

"Oh, that is a sad story that I do not even like to remember, but I will tell you. They had gone out to the camp that day, trying to talk to the other missionary leaders about new ways they could spread the word of God, better ways that would connect people closer to

God. No one listened or cared, they all wanted to do it the same way it had always been done.

Well your parents came back to this very hotel, quite angry and upset that no one would listen to them. That's when your mother and father both broke out in a rare rash. I had never seen anything like it before. Their skin was a reddish color and they were itching profusely, but there was no fever. For days it was like this, the rash spreading over their whole bodies, but no fever. We called for a doctor, and I had both your parents lie down in bed. But by the time the doctor got here your parents were dead. The doctor assumed that it was the cause of some insect bite. Again, the only symptom was a rash and itching for four days, then dead, just gone." Pag's voice was shaky at the end.

Our eyes were welling with tears again, and I let them spill over my cheeks. Why did they have to die, there was so much I wish I could have told them. Almost my whole life they are missing out on. It wasn't fair.

"Pag, do you think my parents are watching me from heaven," I asked starting to cry again.

"Yes dear, I honestly know they are watching you from heaven, every moment. They both loved you so much."

Pag gave me a hug, I hadn't gotten a hug in so long. I felt like a little girl again, when my parents would hug me because I was scared of lightening or such. I wish I could go back there, and tell my parents not to go on that trip to Africa, because they would never come home again.

Chapter 24

curve

For the next two days I stayed in my room. I had all my meals sent up to me. I didn't want to be disturbed. I was writing down everything that Pag had told me. Up until last night I hadn't had a past, and now that I did I wasn't going to take any chance of forgetting it.

The days seemed to be getting longer and hotter. Also, I missed Lief more and more each day that went by. I would replay and replay every touch, every kiss, every word that we had shared together. I hoped by now he had received my letter and was taking it as comfort. I loved Lief, and I wished I was with him now. Oh, let me go home.

I seemed to sigh more these days and my mind always seemed to drift off. I had a brother out there somewhere that I still needed to find. But if Pag knew nothing of him, then who could I expect would? Also, there was Jack, my father, shall I ever meet him? Did I want to meet him? Did he still love my mother?

It was evening time and the dinner bell rang loudly. I hadn't been out of my room in two days, so I decided I would go down to dinner tonight. I entered the dining room with butterflies in my stomach. As I walked to my seat, those who were talking about the weather or such stopped and stared at me. What, did

I really look that much different from everyone else? Until I tell people my name they usually don't pay a bit of attention to me. But then, I get the kind of attention I don't like, the kind that is silent to your face, but loud behind your back.

I sat down at the dining table, it was very large to hold everyone and was round. It was made out of dark wood, very beautiful. On the sides of the table all the way around was a sort of carved pattern in the wood. It was like waves that fell on top of each other, over and over again. I hadn't noticed it before.

The grandfather clock sang in a deep voice that it was now six p.m., time for dinner to be served. Pag's hired African maids came out with plates full of food that looked like they were prepared for the queen herself. It was the only meal that was truly any worth having.

Pag sat down at the head of the table and said grace. We all held hands, except Mrs. Tanna wouldn't hold mine. She blew her nose with her handkerchief before grace was said, then kept her hand by her nose as if she was going to sneeze. Funny really, something that my mother had done over sixteen years ago still bothered people to this day.

After dinner I went back up to my room, when I was about to turn into my room I heard two women talking around the corner. I had to strain my ears to hear and it probably wasn't good of me to listen in on their conversation, but I had to. One voice said, "The nerve of that girl thinking she could hold my hand. I wouldn't touch her filthy hand for all the money in the world."

"Well, they say she is just like her mother.   I wouldn't be surprised if she had five children waiting for her back home, " gossiped another voice.

"Me neither," declared the other.

I could tell that one of the voices was Mrs. Tanna, and from what she said, it was pretty obvious. But I didn't know who the other one was and really didn't care. I was very upset and just felt warm all over. I ran to my room and slammed the door, flopped onto my bed crying and crying. I didn't want to be here anymore, all I wanted to do was go home. Start my life with Lief, that's all.

I'm in a dream.

"Lacy, Lacyyyyyyy," a womans soft voice was calling my name. I was in some field that was covered with dandelions and I was bare naked, but no feeling of concern about it came into my mind.

As I heard my name being called again I awakened from sleeping on the soft grass, my head rose to see who was there. The voice spoke again, "Lacy, you silly thing come hereeeeeeee." The calling was almost in a singing sort of way. I didn't see anyone and it felt like the voice was all around me. The palm trees blew fast in the wind and I could smell the salt from the sea in the air. The sun beat down on my skin and made me feel a perfect, warm feeling. A feeling of gladness I hadn't felt before.

I started walking through the tall grass, not knowing where I was going, but just somewhere.

"Lacy, please come here, you don't understand."

"What don't I understand? Who are you?" I yelled up at the sky, "What do you want?" There was no answer.

95

The wind picked up faster and faster, I shivered and hugged myself trying to keep warm. The wind was sweeping me away, I was falling, being pulled. I tried to fight it, but couldn't. What about the voice? I must find who is saying all these things.

I'm still being pulled, through time it felt. I see faces from home, from school, there's Tabby and Dorothy. I am back in Africa, at that precise moment I fall hard into my bed. There is a loud scream, the voice that was in my dream, it says only, "Wait."

And then I wake up. I'm in a cold sweat but feel totally warm. I am shivering in my sleep, even though my covers are on. I fall back asleep and stay that way the rest of the night. No more dreams, at least that I remember.

Chapter 25

Life

I have decided to write Tabby a letter. She is in England now with Dorothy, but I saw them both in my dream last night and that had reminded me that I had been wanting to write them a letter.

May 1909

Dear Tabby,

I have not written to you in a long time, am hoping both you and Dorothy are doing well. I spent five months on a cargo ship sailing over to Saldahna, South Africa. It was a very long voyage.

I have found out much about my parents and what happened to them, I still have more to uncover. There is a chance that I have a half-brother who is an African. I will write as soon as possible, once I get back to the States, and explain everything.

The weather over here is very hot and dry, it is coolest in the forest where the big leaves hang and give lots of shade.

I hope that you will write to me, but you should probably send the letter to our school. Things can get pretty complicated over here in Africa and I might

> *be gone when the letter finally does reach here. I*
> *plan on going back home soon!*
>   *Please take care.*
>
>   *Love, Lacy*

After I finished my letter to Tabby, I took it to the hotel's front desk to have it mailed as soon as possible. Then I decided to try to find *Madamlee*, who had read my fortune the second day I was here. I needed to ask her something about my brother, maybe she would actually help me this time.

I walked to the spot where her booth had been before, but she wasn't there. I didn't have too many more days left here and I needed to talk to her as soon as possible. I saw Zachin, the young black man who had driven me into the forest that one day. I went to him and asked him if he knew were *Madamlee* was.

"She does not set up her work every day, I bet she would be at her home right now," said Zachin.

"Well, could you take me there?" I asked.

Zachin had a look on his face of uncertainty, "Where I would be taking you, not a lot of white folks live, actually none do."

"That's fine with me," I replied confidently.

Zachin stared at me, then gave a slight smile. He helped me into the carriage and we rode off in the opposite direction from where the missionary camp was. Dust kicked up behind us as we trudged along the dirt roads. I was just thankful there wasn't a wagon in front of us to get dust into our eyes, the heat was bad enough.

It felt like it took quite some time to finally get to the village were *Madamlee* lived. When we arrived, I was the odd duck out of the group. The black children who had just been playing and running around like all children do, stopped in mid game to look at me. I thought it was probably my clothes, maybe they had never seen a dress in that style before. Most of them were just wearing fabric wrapped around themselves, and the littlest children were naked.

"She lives in that hut, last one at the end," Zachin said, pointing to a brown hut made out of dried leaves.

I looked to where he pointed, those butterflies were invading my stomach again. Walking up to her hut, I knocked on the old broken down, wooden door.

"You hellions! I told you to go play outside and not to bother me," said a woman's stern voice from inside.

"Aaaa, ma'am, it's Lacy Slucipher. You told my..." before I could finish *Madamlee* had opened the door. There she stood, not as dressed up as she was before, but still in wild colors.

"Yes dear, come quick," she said, pulling my arm to get me inside and closing the door behind us. "Please, sit."

"Aaa, thank you," I replied, a bit startled.

"So, what can *Madamlee* do for you today?" She said her name as if she were a Greek goddess.

"Well, when you contacted my parents, you would not tell me about my past. Now I have found out the truth and I have another question to ask you."

"Yes?" Her eyes lit up as she leaned towards me.

"I need you to contact my half-brother and tell me, please, where he is so I can find him." I started shaking.

"Oh, aaaa, I do not think I need to do any magic powers to contact your brother," she whispered in a mysterious way.

"What?" I was appalled and stood up quick. "I came asking if you can help me. Why, whenever I ask you for help, do you never give it?" She just looked up at me, and I knew that probably had not been the smartest thing to have said. I sat back down, calmly and didn't say another word.

"If you had let me finish, I would have told you I do not need magic to tell you where your brother is," she whispered again, leaning closer to me. She paused, then said almost silently, "He is right outside."

"What? I do not understand," I stammered.

"You do know Zachin," she asked with a smile.

I tried to speak, but couldn't. I was breathless at the thought that all this time he was my brother. Right in front of my nose. Just as with Captain Jack being my real father. I must try and pay closer attention from now on. "How do you know," I asked with tears forming in my eyes.

"Dear," she said, touching my cheek softly. "I am *Madamlee*. I know all." This time she didn't say her name with any honor, but more with a mild whisper.

"Go to him child, then return home. There is nothing more here for you to find out." She smiled and I left her hut, crying from all that I knew.

As I walked back to the carriage, I composed myself somewhat. Zachin was petting the horse and whistling some happy tune.

"Are you ready miss," he asked with a smile, helping me into the carriage.

As we began our ride back to town I looked at him, trying to think of what to say, then casually asked, "Zachin, do you have any brothers or sisters?"

"No Miss," he replied respectfully.

I cautiously continued, "I have been told that I have a half-brother." Pausing, I said, "It is you. You are my half brother Zachin."

He smiled, thinking I was teasing him. But I did not smile back. "I do not understand. Is this some joke," he stammered with a decreasing smile.

"No. You see it happened this way. My mother was traveling to…" and I told him the entire story, as it had been told to me. He was silent the whole time I spoke and afterwards for a while too.

"Wow," he quietly said, gazing off.

"Look Zachin, tomorrow I am leaving, traveling back to America. You can come with me if you like," I offered.

He looked at me, straight in the eye and asked, "Come to America?"

"Yes," I said, smiling.

"I do not know. I…, I could not. It is not my world, I would not fit in. But, perhaps later on in my life, maybe when I am old I would consider it. Thank you," he replied gratefully.

I smiled and looked down at the ground that was moving under us. We had almost arrived back to town, and it was already rapidly getting dark. I felt nervous and not sure what to say.

"Where do you live? How old are you?" I finally asked.

"Well, since I was a tiny baby I have lived with some people outside of the village. They are my parents and have raised me. I am seventeen, just. You?"

"I am sixteen, so you are about a year older than me. "So," I stalled, "are you married?" It was a normal enough question, he was my brother after all and I thought I had a right to know if my own brother was married or not.

"No, not yet, in a year or so though," he said, smiling at me. It was a relief to see him smile. "Are you," he asked.

"No, I am not married, but I am engaged. His name is Lief Phelpsson, I miss him terribly."

"What does he look like?"

"He," I had to stop and think, I hadn't seen him in such a long time. "He has short blonde hair, and glasses. Is about your height actually. You remind me of him in some ways." We both smiled and rode the rest of the way back to town in silence, but not ackward silence.

It was pretty dark once we got back to town. Zachin brought me to my hotel and told me he would come back in the morning. He would take me to the dock where I would board ship. I was going home.

Chapter 26

flies

Once inside the hotel, I hurried to the front desk. "Pag, I have wonderful news, I must tell you." I was grinning a mile wide. She came around the counter, we walked into the parlor and sat down on the sofa.

"I have found my brother!"

"Really! Who? Do I know him?" She was smiling now too, and I felt like we were two school girls telling each other which boy we fancied.

"It is Zachin, the carriage boy who drove me to the missionary camp that first time and to *Madamlee's* house today. I remember when I first asked Zachin for a ride and told him my name, he said, 'you wouldn't be related to', but he never finished the sentence. He told me that he had heard my last name many times, and felt it always seemed like it was a part of him somehow. And now we both know the truth, I told him the whole story." I was gleaming at this point and talking faster than I normally would.

"Oh honey," Pag gave me a big hug. "I am so glad for you. It's about time you knew the truth. So, how much longer are you staying here?"

My smile faded. "I am planning on going home tomorrow," I said with an unsure voice, realizing that my voyage home would take another long, five months, and that I would have been away from Lief for over a year. A year can take a toll on someones heart. Perhaps he has grown weary of the long wait, found a new love. I worried over this for a while, then came to my senses. Lief told me he loved me, that is what I have to keep my faith in.

Pag just sat there a minute, then said softly, "Well, I am so glad that I got to meet you, the daughter of a very special lady, you always remember that. Your mother was beautiful inside and out, just like you." Her eyes started to get glossy, she hugged me again and then we said good night.

I went to my room and slept peacefully the whole night through. No scary dreams to make me question a part of my life. I hope they never come back. I don't like the feeling of being scared to sleep, it is the only time one is allowed to get away from the bad things in life. Not enter into them.

The next morning came and I woke up with the sun. I packed my belongings carefully, checking every drawer to make sure nothing was forgotten. It was not like I could just sail over here real fast if a bloomer or some other thing was left behind.

Before leaving my room I took one last look around, to try to remember what it had looked like, so I could describe it to Lief and everyone I knew. Stepping to the window sill I moved the lace curtain aside and looked down on the street. The farmers, bakers and fishermen had just begun to set up their market booths, the sea glistened from the rising sun way out at the horizon. I took a mental photograph of everything I saw at that moment, then just walked away.

Carefully trudging down the stairs with my luggage, and having much difficulty I must add, especially with a long, flowing dress on, I passed a mirror and saw that the bun I had put my hair into was about to fall out. I looked ragged. Reaching the front desk was a relief as I set my heavy bags down, then tried to fix my hair. The hotel clerk came out as I rang the desk bell.

Still slightly out of breath I asked, "Could I please send a telegram?"

"Yes. Where to Miss," he asked while picking up paper and pencil from his desk, preparing to write.

I began, *"New York City, America. To Master Lief Phelpsson."*

"And the message ma'am?"

I paused, not sure what to say. *"Boarding ship today, coming home."* I guessed that pretty much covered it.

"And, Ma'am would you like me to call a carriage for you?"

"No, thank you, I have already arranged for someone to pick me up."

"That's fine, ma'am." He smiled, his white, white teeth appearing shockingly from his dark skin. I smiled and turned around to sit in one of the chairs to wait for Zachin to come.

"Lacy darling, I was afraid I might miss you," said Pag, coming around the corner. I stood up in her sudden presence and she gave me a nice hug. "Dear, I will miss you so much."

"I will miss you too, you must come and vist me in New York. I plan on getting married soon, so when we have our own home you can stay with us as long as you want."

"You are getting married? To who?"

"I didn't tell you," I asked, pulling out a picture of Lief to show her. "His name is Lief Phelpsson." I couldn't help but smile, I always did when I talked about him. I expect that is a good thing.

"Oh Lacy, he is so handsome, and I will take you up on your offer to visit. I do not know when, but make sure to send a telegram the minute you are married." She gave me one last hug and whispered something in my ear, "You are a jewel, nothing less than that. I love you, I will always be here for you." Some tears fell down my hot cheeks.

"Lacy, I will take your bags to the carriage." Zachin had just arrived. I smiled at Pag and told her thank you for everything she had done for my family. I turned and got into the carriage.

Chapter 27

by

Zachin and I talked the whole way to the dock where my ship was waiting to take off in a little while. We talked about everything, our families, our schools. I told him about my dear friends, Tabby and Dorothy and everyone, including my teacher who had thought my poems were bad. But that soon, I would be getting a poetry book of my own published.

He told me that when he was young he had climbed and fallen from so many trees that his mother ran out of cloth to put around his wounds. That made us both laugh. He also told me how he was educated in some English writing, but not much. The missionaries had so many families they were all trying to help that no one person got to be educated for very long. He did, though, learn the language fast. The man he had worked for throughout his childhood was English, so he had grown up with it. Zachin said that it would have been bad, for example, to get fired and not understand, but still show up for work the next day. The job he had to know English for was driving people around. So many English folks came here, mostly missionaries, that he had to know how to talk to them.

We both promised each other that we would write as much as possible, and that it was critical that we stayed in touch. We were all either of us had for family. I asked him if he had ever met or seen our father.

"Unlike you, I have not," he answered.

"Yes, I have seen him, but only as the Captain of a ship, and not as my father." That was fine with me though. I would never know him as my father, but I didn't need to. I would always know him in a way that by talking to him for a life time would never amount to what I felt to be true. I knew that his love for my mother had created me. And his love for a beautiful African had created Zachin. That was enough, because I was so glad to know that no matter where I went in the world, I had a brother. Someone who would be right there when I needed him. Just as when I was in the forest, upset and alone. He was there. That was all I really needed to know in my heart.

Chapter 28

like

The long, five month voyage across the sea was a treacherous one, but I was so glad to be on my way home. The ship's captain was a man named, Stew Opanelle. The ship's name was the *Graceful Sage*. A beautiful name I thought. There were still the gross sailors, which I avoided better this time than last, and there were more families aboard too.

The Danielson's and the Franzez', who I thought were originally from Spain, also the Wallabie's. There were twenty two of us in all. The Franzez family had around ten children, I lost count but knew they all were boys, and all looked pretty much the same. Mrs. Franzez looked stressed most of the time and her hair was always frizzed up from running her hands through it when yelling at her boys. Mr. Franzez seemed to always be following the sailors around asking questions like, "So how does that work?" and "Are you sure that rope shouldn't be tied down?" He really was a funny man and was always very polite to me, but never helped Mrs. Franzez out with the children much. He had a round figure and was losing his hair just in the middle of his head. It was funny to see his dark hair, then a pink bald spot where there was no hair.

The rain hit us in August, September too. Most of October was rainy as well, with a few dry days in between. I stayed in my cabin when the day was rainy, bored to death. Nothing to do at all. I could hear the mothers telling their children stories of magical places where it never rained.

On one of the few dry days, something that I will never forget happened. I was walking along the deck with Mrs. Wallabie, just chatting about the weather and such, when we head a loud smack on the water. The sailors ran towards the railing and looked down at the sea. Mrs. Wallabie and I trotted over with everyone else. There, in the water, was Mr. and Mrs. Danielson. Dead. They'd had no children, just each other.

Upon searching their cabin, the Captain discovered a large supply of Laudanum in their belongings. He supposed that they had been addicted to this medicine, which caused them to halucinate. I heard later that some of the sailors had seen them do an odd thing more than once. They were seen lowering and raising a long rope with a bucket tied at the end into the ocean and pulling up water. Apparently they had been secretly drinking the sea water, which along with the Laudanum affected their mental state. The Captain explained that they had probably opened the railing gate, and in their unstable minds thought that it was another level of the ship, so when they stepped through the opening, they fell into the ocean.

"But why did that kill them," asked Mr. Wallabie. Frankly, I was wondering that myself.

The Captain explained, "They fell from so far up that the impact of falling into the water must have snapped their necks. The sea is a bitch that won't forgive. Oh, excuse me ladies, a witch that won't forgive."

How terrible I thought, and only a few weeks from home too. That event set the mood for the next few days, everyone sulking around. All I could think about was getting off this ship, being home again. How wonderful that sounded, to be home.

As I got to thinking about home, I realized I didn't have a home to go back to. Shortly before embarking on this trip, my great aunt's legal advisors had agreed with me to sell her old, run down mansion due to the expense of the major repairs that were needed to be done on it, along with its decreasing value as each year went by. So, since it had been sold, I was basically homeless. All this time I had been thinking of my room back at the school as my home. But I had graduated so wouldn't be able to live there anymore. I knew that Lief and I were going to be married as soon as I got back, but where did I live in the meantime? This worry and thought filled my mind until we landed, finally, at Rhode Island. It was there I had to take a ferry to the mainland, but that sail only lasted a few hours. Then, I was back at the dock in New York Harbor.

Chapter 29

a

It was early November, the month of my seventeenth birthday. I was tired, worn, and felt like I had lived seven lives in this past year. It was very cold, so much different from Africa. There was snow on the ground, beautiful white flakes were falling. I waited on the dock, holding my luggage and tried to raise my shawl over my head so I wouldn't catch my death. A strong hand took hold of one of my bags. I turned to my left quickly to see who was trying to steal my bag right out of my hand. My voice was gone, it was Lief. He was wearing a fur hat and a long black coat. He smiled and took my bags from my other hand. I just stood there staring at him, trying to remember every feeling at this moment, trying not to cry. The snow continued to fall, a flake fell on my cheek and he removed it with his soft hand, along with a hot tear.

I threw my arms around his neck and he dropped my bags to the ground so he could hug me back. He even lifted me off the ground, his hug was so strong. We kissed fiercely, and people who walked by pointed and stuck their noses up at us. But that didn't matter. I hadn't seen Lief in over a year and I didn't give a damn what anyone thought.

We hugged again, then he pushed me back gently to look at me. His eyes were moving fast, back and forth, capturing how I looked, to see if anything had changed. He smiled and I took his arm. He picked up my luggage and we walked over to his driver and carriage. Luckily, the carriage was enclosed, so it wasn't as cold.

"What did you find out? Tell me everything, from the minute you got there. And how was the voyage over and back? Nothing bad happened, did it?" He was talking fast and our eyes were glued to each other.

I felt a bit overwhelmed but told him the whole story, from beginning to end. I told him of my mother being with child before her marriage, and that whenever I said my name to the local people they had shunned me. I told him all about Pag, how she helped me so much and was a great friend. I told him of the irony of discovering that my driver, Zachin, was actually my half brother.

Lief was pretty much silent the whole time. When I finished, he just said, "Wow! I don't know what to say, Lacy. It is amazing to think you went there and found out your whole past, I can't believe it." I nodded in agreement and blushed at loving the way he said my name.

"I have some news of my own," Lief said, looking down at our feet. "Lacy, my father died."

Hearing those words was like a ton of bricks hitting me full force, I couldn't believe it. "Oh, Lief, I am so sorry. When, how," I asked in a very gentle voice. I knew how it felt when ones parents died.

"It happened not too long after you left, it was a heart attack. Very quick," he quietly said.

"I am so sorry, I don't know what to say. How is your mother taking it?"

"Not good, she just sits in her bedroom, either silent or crying. She is better than she was at first, but not much."

We were both silent, I didn't know what to say. I did notice, though, that we had arrived at his father's house, where Lief now lived. I had never seen it before, but it was huge, white was the color, with dark green trim. The front entrance into the house was magnificent. I felt like I was in the presence of royalty.

"I have something else to tell you," Lief said, seeming a bit more excited. "As you know, we own the biggest publishing company in New York, and since my father's death, I have inherited the entire company."

"Oh Lief, that is great!" We were both smiling as he helped me out of the carriage.

Chapter 30

page

Once we were inside, it seemed my eyes grew to take in all the beautiful things in Lief's parents house. The floor was a beautiful gold and red swirled together color. The walls were a sandy color covered with famous paintings. The Mona Lisa on one wall, Girl with a Pearl Earring on the next, and I think my favorite, the Sistin. I was lost in each picture, trying to visualize the artist doing each brush stroke and what was going through their minds as they painted these masterpieces. Words weren't good enough to describe them. In the middle of the room was a huge marble staircase. It swept around and went to another floor above. I could see a parlor to the left and a library to my right.

"Go ahead," Lief said, in a whisper to my ear.

He must have seen me gawking at the Library. I walked slowly into the room, afraid I might awaken it or something. There were shelves ten feet high, all filled with books. Poetry books, fantasy books, learning books, everything one could possibly need.

Lief came up behind me and whispered in my ear gently, "these are all the books my father and his father ever published." He came around beside me and reached out to the book shelf. He scanned his hand along a section of the books, then pulled one out. It was a blood red, hard back, with gold lettering on the binding. It read,

The Selected Poetry Works of
Lacy Pag Slucipher

Tears ran down my face and I smiled. Speechless.

Lief spoke, "This is my favorite book out of all of them." He smiled and I ran to him, threw my arms around his neck, crying and laughing at the same time.

"Thank you," I managed to whisper, still choked up on how nice and wonderful it all was. He hugged me and I never wanted to let go.

The butler walked in holding my bags, he cleared his throat to announce he was there, "Where should I put Miss Slucipher's bags Sir," he asked in a monotone voice.

I let go of Lief's neck and spoke, "That's right, I do not know where I am going to stay now that I am back."

"We have plenty of guest rooms, it will be like your very own living quarters," Lief smiled at me and I giggled some. The butler left and carried my things to my own room.

"I had better let the school know that I have arrived safely, Mrs. Talbee might worry," I said, kind of panicked.

"Alright, we will send a telegraph as soon as possible," Lief promised as he led me to my room. A maid was already there, unpacking my luggage and putting my clothes away for me. I had never in my life been treated this privileged. I liked it a lot.

Chapter 31

that's

Lief left me alone, so I could change into fresh clothes, and get used to things. There were so many pretty things all over my room.

The enormous bed seemed to be five feet off the ground, well, maybe not five feet, but very high off the ground. It even had stairs to climb into it from. The bed was covered with a beautiful handmade quilt that looked like a garden of flowers. Lief told me his grandmother had made it. It was very fluffy with stuffing too! The dresser was made of cherry wood and was sparkling from being freshly dusted. There was a silver hand mirror, engraved with flowers and leaves all over and around the handle too. It was beautiful. The floor was marble, like downstairs, but a different color. It was black and white, very cool underneath my feet.

The paintings on the walls varied, but most were by Van Gogh, one of my favorites. One painting was of the night sky, another of a pond with lily pads in it. They were all breathtaking. Finally, a place that appreciated fine art. I really wish I could have met Lief's father, he seems to have been an extraordinary man.

My closet was almost as big as my room back at school. I had my own powder room, with a bathtub!

The ceiling was painted with wildflowers growing down the sides of the walls. The flowers were purple and the stems different shades of green.

There was a knock at the door and I opened it to see the butler standing straight and tall with a serious face, just like before.

"Master Lief would like to see you in the parlor if you are finished Miss," he said, looking over my head, at what I don't know.

"What is your name, please," I asked with a smile.

"Chandler, Miss." he answered without feeling.

"Thank you Chandler, and you can tell Lief that I will be right down."

"Yes Miss." He turned and walked away.

I shut the door and laughed a little to myself. I scurried over to the mirror to make sure I looked presentable, then went down the long stairs to the parlor that I had seen when I had first arrived.

Lief was sitting on the sofa reading my poetry book when I entered. "Lacy," he greeted, "I wanted to talk to you." I smiled and sat next to him on the sofa. It seems we were both thinking about the same thing at that moment.

Lief asked, "Remember, before you left, we had decided to get married when you returned home?" He seemed a bit nervous, I thought it was sweet.

"Yes," I answered.

He held my hand and looked at me. "Well, I really want to marry you as soon as possible. I love you, you know that. When you were in Africa, you will never know how much I missed you. I want to spend the rest of my life with you, Lacy." His lips went to my hand

and he kissed it gently, with his eyes still looking at me.

I felt light and nervous, but very sure, all at the same time. I felt like I had that first time he kissed me, or said my name in the way that was more than just a friend.

Then, I let my heart speak to him, "Lief, when I was in Africa my mind constantly went to you and the times we'd had together. I don't think you realize that you are the first person in my life that I feel understands me. I love you Lief, I love you so much." As I spoke, the feeling of my love for him completely filled my body and mind.

"Marry me today," Lief gently whispered.

The *today* part came as a bit of a shock. But, as I sat there, very still, my thoughts all fell into place and I whispered back to him, "Yes."

It will be just us, there is not time to invite anyone. Is that alright with you," Lief asked.

I thought for a moment, then said, "We have no need for anyone else to be here. Let's do this, be married today! But what about your mother?"

He got off the sofa and held out a hand, smiling he said, "Come on, I want you to meet her."

Chapter 32

turned

We walked up the stairs and went down a hallway opposite from where my room was. It was a darker looking hallway. As we approached the door I got a feeling of being scared. I hoped that she didn't start crying or oppose us upon hearing of our plans.

Lief knocked on the door and then opened it. A small woman sat at the far corner by a window, looking at the wall though, and not out the window. Lief walked over and put his hand on her shoulder, she didn't move. It was half dark in her room, all of the curtains were closed and her lights were not on. I stood back, waiting for Lief to motion for me to come forth, and I did when he was ready.

Lief spoke quietly, "Mother, this is my fiancée. Her name is Lacy." His mother didn't do anything. Lief tried again, "Mother," he said, giving her a little shake, "this is my fiancée, her name is Lacy. We are to be married today." His mother moved her head in my direction, she gave a slight smile, then turned away to look at the wall. Lief looked at me, I was frozen and just wanted to get out of there as fast as I could.

After we left the room, Lief said, "The doctor says she is in a state of shock from my father's sudden death. The doctor is worried, if she does not come out of it soon she will develope a mind disorder called Melancholy. I don't know what to think." Lief was shaking his head about the whole thing, and I wasn't sure what to do.

"Lief, your mother will come around. Maybe you should give her something to accomplish every day."

"What do you mean?"

"Well, if you got her a plant that she had to be sure to water every day, that would be a few minutes that she would not be thinking about her husband. Then, every few days give her a few small tasks to complete. I think it might help her."

He pondered the thought, then looked at me and said, "You know, you are right! That would be good for her. Let's try that, starting tomorrow."

We smiled at each other as we walked hand in hand down the stairway. At the bottom of the stairs, Lief pulled me close and quietly asked, "Are you ready? Are you ready to begin our life together?"

Smiling up at him I said, "Yes!"

November 1909

Dear Zachin,

I was just married last week to Lief Phelpsson! He is the man I showed you in the photograph. Please write soon, I miss you.

Your loving sister,
    Lacy Phelpsson

November 1909

Dear Tabby,

Lief and I were married last week. I wish you could have been here, but it was a sudden decision, just the two of us. Write soon, I miss you. Please tell Dorothy my good news!

Love,
    Lacy Phelpsson

November 1909

Dearest Pag,

Lief and I were married last week. I miss you so much and have told Lief all about you. You must come and visit us sometime soon! Please write whenever you can.

Love,

Lacy Phelpsson

November 1909

Dear Mrs. Talbee,

Lief Phelpsson and I have married last week. Please spread the good news around. I will try to come for a visit soon.

Love,

Lacy Phelpsson

Selected Poetry
of
Lacy Pag Slucipher

Tiger Tiger
hear my cry
While running through the
endless time
Hold me tight
and all is right
Tiger Tiger
hear my cry
Find me soon
before I take off
and die

Let go

Sorry I forgave you
Sorry that I let you go
Sorry for cryin
Lets go
Your hands said enough
They were tough, strong, final
I will forgive you but you have to let me know
That you have to let go

To The Sea

Will you take me away
please dear sea
Swallow me whole
and let me feel the need
I asked you before
but you disagreed
Drift me away to something free

Keep to Yourself

Secrets are secrets,
they're not for you to know.
Keep them in your heart
for something real that can flow.
Secrets are secrets,
they're not for you to know.
Like a bond between two friends
nothing else can go.

I'm getting tired,
too tired to be.
I don't know what
I need anymore.
Let me come home,
home to sleep.
I feel like I'm falling
into something deep.

Take this letter and run with it,
see if it will fly.
Throw it up high
and just maybe it will catch fire.
Who knows,
if you take this letter
and run with it.

Hush now
don't say those words
Smile slightly so no one
knows you hurt
Hush now
let yourself calm
Nothing's the matter
and nothing's wrong

Why won't you be my friend
I gave you big smiles that never end
Why won't you be my friend
Is it something that I said
or is it just because you're sad
Why won't you be my friend
I promise you can carry on
until we both feel dead
Why won't you be my friend
I'm not so weird once you understand

Dearest,
I have gone away
passed onto the dead
I hopefully didn't
leave anything in dread
I have seen the sun
rise and fall
I have seen the moon
cradled in the gloom
But your face I will
never see again
And that is what pains me
to the end.

Epilogue

The school Lacy attended as a young girl continued as a girls school for many years after her graduation. It was awarded one of the best schools for girls in the country in 1915. It is no longer functioning, but has been turned into a museum.

Caitlina, the young girl who had fits that only Lacy could calm down, grew up to be a world famous actress. Her main roles were dramatic scenes, involving crying, screaming and throwing fits, just like when she was a little girl. She never forgot Lacy though, and the kindnesses Lacy had shown her.

Tabby, Lacy's best friend who had moved to England with Dorothy, stayed there her whole life. She only visited Lacy one time after moving there, but they wrote to each other often over the years. Tabby became a singer at local events in her village. Dorothy became a specialist of the mind, one of the few women in her class. Neither of them ever married, but always remained friends.

Zachin lived in Saldanha, South Africa until he was very old, then died one day when working out in his wheat field. Lacy never got to see him, except for the one time when she first found out he was her half brother. Lacy and Zachin wrote back and forth over the years. Zachin married a childhood friend and they had five children. Lacy was proud to be their aunt, and always remembered them on birthdays and holidays by sending them expensive gifts. And even though they never got to meet their Aunt Lacy, they kept in touch with her by writing letters often. Lacy loved Zachin very much, she didn't even have a picture of him, but knew in her heart what he looked like.

Lief's mother slowy, day by day, became happy with life again. She took up a hobby of planting and growing flowers and vegetables and spent her days enjoying life in her garden. Many people would say that when passing by the Phelpsson house you always knew if she was gardening that day or not, because if she was you could hear her humming a happy tune.

Lacy never saw Captain Jack Follow, her birth father, again. She never really regretted not knowing her birth father, he was always someone she could dream about on a rainy day. She felt that sometimes it was better to know a person by what you think they are like, and not necessarily by what they truly are like.

Lacy went on to have three more volumes of poetry published, and one novel that won five awards. It was about her life when she was a young girl at school, and when she traveled to South Africa to find out the truth about her past.

Lief was always very proud of the things that Lacy accomplished. He went on running the publishing business that still today is the top publisher in New York.

Lacy and Lief had three children, two son's and a daughter. The oldest was named Carl Jack Phelpsson. They named him after Lacy's two fathers. Their youngest son was named after Lief's father, Alonso Lief Phelpsson. And their daughter was named Pagena

Saldanha Phelpsson in honor of Lacy's dear friend Pag of Saldanha, Africa.

The family lived in Lief's childhood home, which was left to him upon his mother's death. The family business was passed onto one of the children. It was supposed to go to the oldest son, but as you know rules don't always need to be followed. Sometimes good things will come out of it, even if the rules are broken.

About the Author

Karla Gustafson has always written and created stories. Even before she could write, she dictated them to her Mom, who would write them down for her. In the last three years Karla has written numerous songs and over 300 poems, a few of which were published in youth magazines and the "Best Poems and Poets of 2003" book.

Karla attends high school and lives with her parents and older brother in Oregon.

Printed in the United States
28122LVS00001B/64-81

9 781420 833430